STO

WESTERN STORIES

ALLEN COUNTY PUBLIC LIBRARY

3 1833 01161 1123

SO-BKS-753

The Trail to Lost Horse Ranch

THE TRAIL TO LOST HORSE RANCH

Archie Joscelyn

AVALON BOOKS

THOMAS BOUREGY AND COMPANY, INC.
22 EAST 60TH STREET • NEW YORK 10022

© Copyright 1977 by Archie Joscelyn

PUBLISHED SIMULTANEOUSLY IN THE DOMINION OF CANADA
BY GINN AND COMPANY, SCARBOROUGH, ONTARIO

PRINTED IN THE UNITED STATES OF AMERICA
BY THE COLONIAL PRESS INC., CLINTON, MASSACHUSETTS

For
George Harper

L 1949193

1

Frustration and a nagging sense of ill-being had bothered McKay for weeks. Big Mac to his friends, even tempered and often jovial, he was conscious that others had taken to eyeing him furtively, and he could hardly blame them. Irritation burst from him as he banged down his coffee cup and scraped back his chair. His bellow brought the cook in a hurried scurry, apprehension widening his closely set pale eyes.

"What the devil's the matter with this coffee, Shaney?" McKay demanded, the sleeplessness from a persistent headache pinching his face and jaw. Recently nothing was exactly wrong, while everything seemed to be. He was prey to nameless irritations, none of which he could quite pin down. But the coffee was bitter, tangibly vile.

"It tastes like the sweepings from a stable," he growled. "Don't you ever scour the pot? I'd as soon drink bilge water."

"C-coffee, Mr. McKay?" Shaney's too-pale skin had gone almost yellow. "Y-you say it tastes bad? I'm sorry. But you never complained before—"

He had become known as Big Mac as much from overlooking small irritations as from his size and steadiness of purpose. Consciously now he forced a grip upon himself.

"I've felt like it. It's terrible stuff. I think I'll go back to eating with the rest of the boys. Maybe I need a change from my own company," he added dourly. "Or yours," he amended under his breath, with a sudden surge of dislike for the hasher. The man could cook—but so could a fox preen in the sun, move among a flock, and turn suddenly to slash a throat.

The boys . . . Increasingly he had lost touch with them, isolated first when a badly sprained ankle had confined him to the house for weeks. Somehow the custom of eating in the kitchen had been established. Turning, he scooped a battered hat from a wall peg, again aware that his grab for it was a little off-target. At first it had been irritating. All at once it was frightening, as were so many small things that he had always until then taken for granted.

Outwardly there was little difference between himself, owner of Lost Horse Ranch, and his foreman, Baldy O'Brion, or any of the hands. Still, with privileges went responsibilities. As Big Mac, he had more or less clawed his way to the top, building Lost Horse from a dubious inheritance to the supreme ranch on the range, and McKay, while younger than most of those who took his pay, was separated from them by a subtle but clear line.

Makepeace McKay had been a dreamer rather than a manager. Strong men both, father and son had clashed over the need for building up the outfit instead of adding to the already oversized sprawl of a house. Rather than openly bicker, Dave had found a job on a distant spread, returning at a sudden summons after half a dozen years to find himself the owner of a heavily mortgaged and faltering cattle outfit. He could only stare in appalled disbelief at the additions to the great house—its lower story of logs, the upper framed, vast and splendid in the middle of nowhere—himself, like his father before him, its only occupant.

Makepeace had lavished money, time, and

effort on his hobby, leaving his acres neglected. Within a few years Big Mac had paid off the debts and enlarged the herds. In the process, by right as well as custom, he had become the Old Man, and his crew liked him well enough—at least some of them. But now and again he sensed resentment at the change from the old, easy-going ways.

Well, to the devil with those who might disagree. A boss had to be on top of his job, always in command. He must maintain control not only of circumstances but of himself. A subtle unease that he might be losing that control had begun to nag, like a buzzing fly penned and frantic in a closed room. Suppose his aim should be off, if he had to use his gun—by no more than a fraction, but like his grab for his hat? It was like going down stairs and stepping confidently, only to find that the step was missing.

Jamming the hat on his head, he stepped out, glaring back at the early morning sunshine slanting at him across the roof of the combined bunk- and cookhouse. Big as it was, it was dwarfed by the monster of a house behind.

Instead of turning for the barn, as he had intended, McKay jerked open the door to the long dining room and stepped through, conscious of the sudden pause of the men at table, the lifting heads and turning eyes. Somehow he had become almost a stranger, an interloper on his own ranch.

"Hi, boys," he said, managing to make it sound casual. "Thought I'd say hello. Drink a cup of coffee with you."

Baldy O'Brion's eyes smiled even as they seemed to narrow. The foreman's aspect was as deceptively meek as it was benign, the fringe of curly hair with shining baldness above lending almost a cherubic appearance. His surprise was masked beneath lowering lids. He offered an empty cup with one hand and seized the big pot from table's end with the other, pouring and shoving it forward in a long, smooth motion.

"Nothin' like good Arbuckle to start a day." He nodded. "And Shaney makes good coffee."

Drinking, McKay nodded agreement. This was more like it. What the smaller pot needed, of course, was a good scouring. He threw a leg across the corner of the table, lounged, and visited. He'd keep on with them, though for today he had business in town.

Tomorrow, he resolved suddenly, he would take a break, head out with a pack horse for the back country for a few days of fishing and taking things easy. That was probably what ailed him, driving too hard. What was the use of being the boss if you couldn't take a vacation when you wanted one?

This time, he sure enough would take a rest—get rid of nameless imaginings and headaches and all the rest. He was suddenly eager.

2

Longpre Connor, his bare bald head and ragged
beard increasing his usual hungry resemblance to a
buzzard, was returning home to his ranch much as
he had done on most Saturdays for nearly a score
of years. He maintained a comfortable if not quite
dignified stance in the saddle, clinging owlishly to
the saddle horn with one hand while holding the
reins with the other. Long practice had rendered

him adept at the twenty-mile ride through dark of night and in all sorts of weather.

The chief share of credit for such accomplishments belonged not to Longpre but to the horses who carried him. Eager for their own stable, they were more competent and trustworthy than Longpre himself. A buckskin cayuse had done its job for more than a decade. Since then, Longpre had entrusted himself to a calico pony. The ears of each animal were trained to disregard the lachrymose sounds from Connor that passed for song.

Always upon reaching the stable door the pony halted, and Longpre, rousing from somnolence, shouted for assistance from one of the men asleep in the bunkhouse. Having aided him off the horse and in to the house, the hand cared for the patient pony and another weekly ritual was over.

But today there had been a difference. Calling as usual for the ranch's mail when he reached town, Connor had been both shocked and surprised to find a letter addressed to himself. The handwriting was unfamiliar but almost certainly that of a lady. The postmark was of a small town on the eastern seaboard. Even before opening it, Longpre sensed that it contained trouble.

Once read, his worst fears had been confirmed. Fears which, over a score of eventless years, had gradually faded until they had been all but forgotten. Suddenly they were revived, even more unpleasantly than he had expected.

The letter began on a note of formality.

Dear Mr. Connor,

I scarcely know how to address you, a man even of whose existence as a living being I knew nothing at all until a very few days ago, much less that you were—or should I say are?—my father.

My mother supported and cared for me all my life. Twenty years in which, while not actually being told as much, I had assumed that she was a widow. Only when she knew that she was dying did she break her self-imposed silence to reveal what she had learned from various sources—first that you were alive; also to inform me that you are my father, proprietor of a cattle ranch purchased long years ago with money my mother had inherited from *her* father.

She told me of the disagreement that led to the parting between the two of you—you being determined to head west for California and the Gold Rush, following what you believed a certain road to great wealth, but a course that she considered both foolish and hazardous. With the result that you, along with my brother Ashley, four years older than I, set off—she called it sneaking away—in two days, taking nearly all her money with you.

You never wrote, nor returned any sort of message in all the years since. But by dint of correspondence and inquiry Mother learned finally how, instead of continuing on to California, you had changed your mind and bought a ranch, and how you have apparently done quite well as a stockman, prospering to at least a reasonable extent.

After the fashion in which you deserted her, she was always too proud to write or seek you out, even when her health failed and her small remaining resources were exhausted. But when she realized that she had only a few days to live, she told me these things and pointed out that I am your daughter and so doubly entitled (because the ranch was bought with her money) to a share of property and a living.

You will understand that I was both startled and shocked, and not at all eager to make your acquaintance or to press such a claim upon you. But at her insistence that I should, I promised. If this letter seems brutally frank, it appears justified under the circumstances. Still I am mindful that there are nearly always two sides to every story, and

I shall strive to hear your side with an open mind, and in the hope that you may find a daughter and I a Father.

I will follow this letter within a few days.

Cleone Connor

Badly shaken, Longpre Connor had sought to lessen the impact at his favorite bar, but was not too successful. Though more drunk than usual, his mind remained active. To any man such a missive might come as a nasty shock. To him, after such a lapse of years, it was, like the name of his ranch, triply so.

With a largely unsuspected, sardonic sense of humor, he had taken for his brand the Three X—a triple cross. And the Triple Cross it had become.

Another shock, of a different nature, awaited. The pony was turning in toward the barn when a startled jackrabbit took off suddenly from almost under its hoofs. The pony jumped and plunged wildly.

Normally, even when well liquored, Longpre Connor could keep his seat on any horse. This time he lost his footing in the stirrups and his hold on the saddle horn. There was no chance to summon assistance.

When he was discovered, after the sun had risen, the exposure following his tumble had worsened an already bad condition. Carried into the house, he realized, as Cleo's mother had done only a few weeks before, that his time was short. Remembering that final promise in the letter—a promise that was almost a threat—he decided that he too had things to tell, a confession to make.

Informed that a cowboy had been dispatched to Rawhide to find and fetch the doctor, Longpre was not impressed. Whatever else he was, he had always been a realist, and never more so than now, with the certainty that he was dying. At the best, assuming that Dr. Slingsby could be found at home or office and make a prompt response, it would be day's end before he could arrive. Longpre did not expect to be around that long.

"It's probably better luck than I'd any right to expect, to go fast," he commented, with a philosophy so unlike him as to betoken the approach of the end. In health he had never been noted for such an attitude. Blinking up at Slash Connor—his son had never been known as Ashley—he found only the blank face and watchful eyes he expected. Slash had his father's height plus added beef and muscle. In some ways they were alike and in others all but strangers.

Across the years there had been little love between father and son. They had clashed increasingly about policy and how the ranch should be run, especially in relation to its big neighbor, the rival outfit of the Lost Horse, whose acres Slash coveted. Already he was gloating in the certainty that the Triple Cross would soon be his.

As cold-blooded as a snake, as savagely ruthless in his manner of striking, it would serve Slash right if Longpre withheld warning of upcoming events, letting him deal with what was slated to happen as best he could. And he would do so, Longpre decided, if Slash alone was involved; it would be a valuable, needed lesson. But with a girl involved, that was different. After enjoying property that was rightfully hers for a score of years, perhaps he owed her something.

With an effort he roused from a half lethargy, his voice little more than a whisper.

"You'll find a letter in my coat pocket," he instructed. "Read it."

Not at all to Longpre's surprise, Slash nodded.

"I have. You're an even bigger scoundrel than I had thought."

"Likely." Longpre had neither the strength nor the desire to argue. "But not quite the way you think. It doesn't matter now what our name used to be, except that it wasn't Connor. Joining the gold rush was convenient in several ways. It was a good place to lose oneself, to hide—which was what I was doing."

His son's face showed no surprise, while his tone was sardonic.

"You mean that you were on the dodge?"

"What else? Anyhow, I had some luck, sort of a mixed bag. We were headed west, right out in the middle of nowhere, when your Ma took sick, like lots of others on that hell trail. Cholera. It was near the same as being hit with an axe. I remember she cooked breakfast that morning, then said she didn't feel like eating. Before suppertime, she was dead."

Slash nodded. He had heard that part of the family history before. Once it had held the power to move him, but not any longer.

"There were others with the wagon train in a similar situation," Longpre went on. "Another outfit, a man and a small boy, had camped next to us. I took notice because his team and wagon were a lot better than mine. Well, they died that same day, along with quite a few others. Of those who survived, most were too scared to look after their sick or bury their dead. All they could think of was to run, as if they could outrun fate when their number was up." His lip curled cynically.

"With all the confusion and nobody interested in anything except saving himself, it was easy to trade outfits. In the other wagon I found some papers and letters. Their name was Connor, so I took that name along with the rest. I figured it wouldn't make any difference to him, and it might to me, in two or three ways.

"I found out that this Longpre Connor had had

different notions from most of the others who'd been heading over that trail. He was going along with the wagon train for a while, since that was the only halfway safe way to travel, but not with the notion of reaching California. Before starting out he'd been having some correspondence with a friend, who had gotten hold of a big parcel of land—just how, I never knew, but anyway, it was this ranch. This friend's health was poor, and he wanted to get away. So he'd sold to Connor, sticking him for a lot more than the place was worth at that time. Anyhow, Connor had been heading for this ranch, with the deed to it and everything in good order, near as I could make out.

"So I took over the ranch as well as the name and the wagon. Since nobody around here had ever seen either of us, nobody asked any questions. It was as simple as that."

Slash listened to the recital with mounting interest. Weak-willed and uncertain of purpose, Longpre Connor—as he'd been for twenty years— had been a poor manager, poorly equipped either by nature or training to handle such an outfit. More than once Slash had wondered how he had ever gotten hold of such a spread. Finally the mystery was explained.

"So he'd pulled out, deserting his wife and

daughter but taking along the son? Is that it? From the sound, he must have been a lot like you. I'd say his wife didn't lose much."

Longpre made a small gesture of dissent.

"You've got him wrong. I guess he wasn't so bad. Sure they'd had words, and he'd taken off to make a new start in fresh country, leaving his wife and daughter behind when she had refused to go along. She thought it was as crazy as it turned out to be. But once he started, he cooled off and had second thoughts. There was a letter in the wagon that he'd written to his wife, but he hadn't had any chance to send it off, he was took so sudden.

"In it he explained about the fine big ranch that he'd been lucky enough to get hold of. Then he went on to say that as soon as he reached it and had things fixed up fit for a woman, he would send for her and their girl. He pointed out that though she'd been dead set against him prospecting, she had liked the idea of a farm, so to please her he'd come around to that notion, though it was a cattle ranch instead of a corn and chicken farm."

Slash grunted, only mildly interested. All those matters were far in the past, and the recital elicited neither his sympathy nor concern, save insofar as this new letter was from the small daughter, now grown to womanhood. That such an heir to the property was alive and on her way to the country might complicate matters, just when fate had arranged for him finally to come into the owner-ship.

"It will be a damned nusiance if she shows up," he observed, speaking his thoughts aloud. "I take it that you never sent that letter that her pa had written?"

"Would I be such a fool?" his father countered. "I never figured that anybody could trace them or me. It seems now that my mistake was in taking that name, for somehow or other they have run it down. But at the time it seemed necessary as well as a good idea. Now—well, it'll be up to you."

Slash stared thoughtfully from the window.

"If it wasn't that I'm supposed to be her long-lost brother, I might marry her. That would fix everything up legal for both of us. But as it is— what a blasted mess!"

Longpre nodded. "I reckon so. But you'll have to handle it. I won't be here to help. Only when she gets here, treat her as if she was your sister. She's got that much coming to her."

Slash nodded. "Sure." He swung away from the window, speaking somberly.

"I'll be busy with the ranch. In any case, I don't war on women—though if she has notions about grabbing off half the place, she could be asking for trouble."

3

Cleo Connor, stepping down from the weariness of endless miles by stagecoach, felt a mixture of expectancy and excitement as she stood, looking about. This town of Rawhide, even to its name, was in many respects similar to others she had passed through in the last few days. Its main and only real street loomed with false-fronted buildings, most of them unpainted or peeling. The number of saloons, which alone had a certain air of prosperity and legible signs, equalled or outnumbered the other business enterprises. In the background a few houses huddled.

There was one thing that made Rawhide different. Besides being the nearest town to the ranch of which she was rightfully the part-owner, Rawhide possessed a sawmill. The pungency of sawdust and rosin came pleasantly on the air.

Lost Horse Creek swung out from timbered hills to the north to alternately swirl and hesitate at the edge of the town. The mill was a contrast in colors to the browning landscape, with logs stacked along the banks or floating in the dammed-up pond above. Below were piles and tiers of fresh sawed boards and planks imparting their own rosinous fragrance.

A faint frown appeared between Cleo's blue eyes as the driver snapped his whip half in salute and the stage departed. Aside from a few wondering or speculative glances cast her way, no one had appeared to welcome or even show an interest in her arrival. Somehow, despite past years and the uncertain history, she had expected at least to be met. After making full allowance for past difficulties and such a lapse of time, a father should at least be hospitable. She had counted on that.

But no one had come, and she was clearly on her

own. On the small side, Cleo stood straight, determined to appear taller, eyes not only wide-set but wide-open and undaunted. But she looked uncertainly at the bulging carpetbag and small, leather-bound trunk that appeared as out of place as herself. They were the last links with the life she had known and from which she was removed not merely by thousands of miles but in countless other ways, including lack of money. Something akin to dismay made the breeze blow cold.

She clenched her small fists, and a single freckle alongside a slightly up-tilted nose showed with sudden prominence. Drawing a deep breath, she entered the stage station and questioned the little man who seemed almost to teeter on a high stool. He reminded her of a gopher, but the pale, watery eyes, peering above steel-rimmed spectacles, expressed concern.

"Why no, miss, I ain't seen nothin' of anybody from the Triple Cross, not today. You say you thought they'd meet you? You just out from the east? Might be your letter was delayed, or something—"

"I sent it so that it should have arrived well ahead of me," Cleo protested. Half consciously she took note of his reference to Triple Cross. Her term had been the Three X.

"We-el—" Darrigan's eyes brightened behind thick lenses as he descended from the stool.

"Seems like there's been a mix-up somewhere. That would be it, of course, what with Longpre Connor's funeral only yesterday, so with matters more or less at odds and ends out there—"

"Funeral, did you say? Longpre Connor?" Her voice was between gasp and surprise.

"Why, yes. Longpre Connor was buried yesterday, or so I heard tell. Died from an accident. You all right, miss?"

"Yes, I—I'm fine," Cleo assured him, white teeth suddenly against lower lip. The news was an explanation, but a shocking one. To come so close to meeting and knowing her father, only to miss him in such fashion! She had envisioned all sorts of possibilities but not that.

Still, even if he was dead, her own situation was unaltered. She had a brother; she was rightfully the half-owner, at the least, of the ranch; and more to the point, she had nowhere else to go.

Though not giving her name or reasons, she made it clear that she had come a long way to visit at the ranch and was more than ever anxious to reach it. The little man rubbed an earlobe reflectively, staring along the nearly deserted street. Suddenly his glance brightened.

"Maybe this can be worked out. See that wagon? Load of lumber. Dave McKay drivin' it, and he's headin' back for his own ranch. It's—it—"

He hesitated, suddenly recollecting the long-standing bad-feeling between the two big outfits. Then he went on doggedly.

"Dave's place is the Lost Horse. Adjoins the Triple Cross. Reckon he'd be more'n pleased to give a lady a lift out to where you want to go. It'll be about the only likely chance for a ride. I'll ask him."

Not waiting for consent, he scurried to mid-street, dust plopping in small gusts beneath his feet, and hailed McKay with a shrill soprano. McKay, handling the reins of a four-horse team from the seat of the lumber wagon, pulled to a stop, a friendly smile spreading the great thicket of freckles that adorned his cheeks. Thought of the vacation he had promised himself had gone far to mellow his mood and dispel his doubts. That was what he needed, just a few days of rest and fishing.

Cleo noticed the wideness of the shoulders, the tallness of the man even as he sat. Half-consciously it came to her that he was what she had always pictured a westerner to be.

"Howdy, Dave," Darrigan hailed. "Got a sort of favor to ask of you. No, I ain't either," he amended. "Reckon it's the other way, if anything. Little lady here's just got off the stage, all the way from down east. Figured to be met but wasn't. Wants to get out to Connor's place. Since that's out your way, maybe you could give her a lift."

McKay gave her a second and closer appraisal.

His eyes held only guarded approval, with no hint of surprise that such a woman, obviously a lady, should have such a destination in mind. More observant than his lounging air indicated, he was struck by the paleness of her cheeks, as though she had sustained a shock, and then he realized that the news of Longpre's death might have had an unsettling effect.

Triple Cross adjoined his own ranch but was closer to town. But to swing off from the main road and take a passenger in to the ranch house on Connor's would add half a dozen miles, which with so heavy a load was considerable. But he gave no inkling of that as he doffed his hat in grave salute.

"This wagon seat ain't the most comfortable place to ride, ma'am—but if you'd care to accept such accommodations, why, you're more'n welcome."

Cleo accepted promptly. Not only was it increasingly apparent that she was not going to be met by anyone from Three X, but in view of the recent death there, a mix-up was understandable. And while a wagon, heavily laden and slow-moving, was not the sort of transportation she had envisioned, she liked this man who would be her neighbor. That the wizened clerk clearly vouched for him was an added reason.

Dave McKay wrapped the reins around the brake handle after kicking it hard in place. He came down over a wheel, lifted her baggage up, then hesitated.

"I usually get a cup of coffee and a bite to eat before I start the trip back," he lied easily. "Maybe you could stand a bite along with me." Refreshment and a few minutes' rest would be welcome after any stage ride. And if he was any judge, she would need to be well fortified for what might lie ahead.

The coffee, he noted almost absently, was good. But that was secondary to the companionship of such a woman.

Outside again, McKay lifted her up with the same ease he had shown with her trunk, untied the team, and put them to a trot. Cleo felt a little breathless.

"This is very good of you, Mr. McKay. Though if we're neighbors, perhaps it's not too much out of your way."

"Nothing to worry about," he assured her, casting a quick eye at the sun. Instead of getting back by sundown, it would be moonrise before he returned from dropping her off. But he definitely did not mind.

"I suppose you're wondering who I am and why I arrived in such fashion," Cleo said as the town fell behind. "I've always lived with my mother, until her—her passing, a short while ago. I had more or less taken it for granted that my father had died while I was a baby. Then I learned that I had a father and a brother out this way, and that my mother's money had been used to pay for the ranch. So I wrote ahead, then set out; and here I am. It still seems unbelievable, even to me."

"It must have been upsetting, especially to get off the stage and learn that your father had just been buried," McKay conceded. However odd, it was possible, and he had no doubt that she was telling the truth. But how she could be sister to such a man as Slash Connor was hard to understand. As for the lack of anyone to meet her, that might be due to the confusion of recent events. On the other hand, the news of such a relationship had probably been as big a surprise to Slash as it was to her. Coming with a claim to at least part ownership of Triple Cross would hardly ensure a welcome. The oversight at town could well be deliberate.

"I can't honestly pretend to much grief for a father I never knew," Cleo went on. "Especially since he took so little interest in either me or my mother. Oh, I'm sorry—I forgot to tell you my name. It's Cleone. Cleo for short."

"Cleo." McKay repeated thoughtfully. "Kind of unusual—but mighty pretty."

"Thank you. I—I'm hoping, of course, that I'll like my brother, and that it will be mutual. After such a long while, and all the wasted years—well, they seem so useless, so—so futile."

Finding no reply, McKay clucked to the team, who had slowed, taking advantage of a momentarily lax hand on the reins. Cleo noticed that he offered neither suggestion nor reassurance in regard to what she might find.

"Do you know what happened to my father?" she asked. "Somehow it seems so terrible, after such a long time, to come and then miss him by only a couple of days."

McKay offered no condolences, contenting himself with answering her question.

"I heard that he had a fall from his horse and was hurt bad. Lived only a few hours."

Cleo gave a soft cluck of distress. That seemed to explain a lot, atoning for any oversight regarding her arrival.

"How awful! I could scarcely have arrived at a worse time, could I? Were you at the funeral?"

"No. It was private."

That seemed somehow strange. He was a next-door neighbor, and she had heard much of the friendliness and companionship of the west. Even strained relations were forgotten at such times. And to hold a private rather than public funeral! After so many years, Longpre Connor should have been well known.

"I suppose both ranches—yours and the Three X—are large ones?" she probed in a growing uncertainty.

"Pretty big," McKay acknowledged. "They both take in some public land." He gestured toward the north. "That's Triple Cross—everything along here on that side of the road."

Cleo, despite the open country and vast distances to which she had grown accustomed from the stage, gasped. She surveyed the land with growing interest. It looked empty of any signs of occupancy.

"You mean we're almost there?"

"Nope. The buildings on Triple Cross are about twenty miles out from town. Connor—your father—he figured it as just a nice week-end ride. Quite a way yet."

"I suppose so." Her voice was small. "And your place—how far is it between the houses on the two ranches?"

"About fifteen miles—less as a crow flies, or would be if he held straight."

And he was the next-door neighbor! From her experience, a neighbor was no farther than across a street. As if reading her mind, McKay posed a question.

"You do any horseback riding?"

"A lot." Cleo laughed suddenly. "I love to ride, and I can see where knowing how will come in handy. Is that what you were thinking?"

"Sort of. Being a good rider is useful out here." He let it go at that. In the careful manner with which he skirted the subject, she was increasingly certain that while the owners of these two big ranches might be neighbors, they were not friends. Neither he nor apparently any other outsiders had attended the funeral. That told its own story. She shivered.

McKay was instantly solicitous. "Are you cold? I'll rustle up a blanket for a robe—"

"No, I'm not cold," Cleo denied. "It was . . . involuntary." Riding the train for more than half the journey west, she had forced herself to be open-minded, to realize that there might have been, indeed must have been, fault on both sides. Her mother, feeling herself and Cleo deserted, defrauded, and neglected, had had reason for prejudice. But she had heard only one side of the story. It would be only fair, as well as sensible, to give her father and brother a chance to tell theirs.

But everything that she was hearing now tended to reinforce her mother's attitude. Longpre Connor clearly had been on unfriendly terms with his neighbors. At a funeral, even enemies tended to look for good in the departed, to let bygones be bygones.

Determinedly she changed the subject. She gathered that McKay was a bachelor, busy with running his ranch, taking home lumber for repairs to his house.

"It's a big affair and takes some keeping up," he explained.

The sun was close to setting when he indicated a

huddle of buildings—a long, squat log house, a vastly bigger barn, looking almost as deserted as the surrounding countryside.

"Must not have got your letter, from the looks of things," he observed. "It hardly seems like you're expected."

4

It was easy to tell himself that he was more pleasantly excited than he had been for a long while because he was going off for a few days of good fishing and a real vacation, alone. That was a part of the yeasty state of his mind, but McKay realized that some of it stemmed from the direction he was taking, a swing that would bring him within sight of a big section of Triple Cross;

territory adjacent to his own land, likely country, if she should be inclined for a ride, and what could be more natural?

Color rushed beneath his tan, intensifying his freckles. Even if he should catch a glimpse of her at a long distance, she would be unlikely to see him. And in any case, why should she be interested, since he had only given her a ride out from town?

Such notions were foolish if not fantastic. More and more, of late, he was beginning to wonder if he were quite rational. Certainly a lot of crazy ideas kept popping in and out of his mind.

But he held the course, even though it added some miles to his planned ride. After all, he had plenty of time, and some of these more remote parts of the range could stand a closer look. They were so far off and hard to reach that they were visited but rarely by himself or any of his crew. Checking on any stock that might have strayed to such recesses was a good idea.

His thoughts swung back to Cleo. That such a girl could be the daughter of Longpre Connor or sister to Slash was more fantastic than the notions that sometimes troubled him, but apparently it was so. He wondered how the situation would work out. At his hail, Slash had appeared, staring with surprise and hostility, then advancing to greet Cleo politely but not warmly. McKay had hated to go on and leave her. But it was not his business, and Slash, at least, wouldn't welcome any interference in either his ranch or his affairs, especially by him.

For half an hour of riding, McKay had a good view of distant but empty country—empty except for occasional grazing cattle. But after days of train and stage, she would hardly want any more riding for a while.

A small tributary of the Lost Horse faltered its way among the hills, and his horse stopped to drink. The pack horse took advantage of the opportunity to brush against a tree in hopes of rubbing loose its burden. At his sharp command it sidled resignedly into the stream and lowered its head, then jerked it up so suddenly that water dribbled from its lips. McKay's mount caught a scent and danced, hoofs muddying the creek bottom. But there was nothing to see, no taint or fragrance on the wind that McKay's more poorly attuned sense could pick up. Presently, moving on, the horses lost their fright.

McKay stared, surprised. In the sandy soil were the imprints of horses' hoofs, shod tracks, and not many days old. Coming upon such a trail was as odd as it was unexpected. His curiosity stirred, he swung his pony to follow the sign. They climbed a slope, then dipped. The trail held straight, despite hampering brush and obstacles causing brief detours. It was not quite a trail, yet more than a trace, as though the same path had been taken on more than one occasion.

McKay's nostrils wrinkled to an alien odor, faint but pervasive. He was at a loss to identify it, though this time the horses were untroubled. Then, pushing through a screen of close-set trees, they emerged into the sunshine of a small, remote meadow. At its far edge were signs of human activity.

Two boulders, gray-green in the sun, each as big as a good-sized room, leaned with their tops against each other, like building blocks dropped and forgotten. The inverted V beneath them formed a natural room. Not far to the side, the creek slid past.

Dismounting, McKay explored, torn between interest and surprise. Under the cover of the rocks was a still. There was no mistaking the boiler, the coils of pipe. A considerable stack of dry wood was piled nearby for fuel. Under the boiler were dead ashes.

What struck him as odd was that there was no odor of liquor, only another elusive, somehow disturbing scent. Discovering a sort of path, he followed it to a sodden pile of still moist, discarded refuse. The stuff reminded him of the pigweed his mother had gathered and cooked for early greens—lamb's quarters, as his father had insisted was the proper name. This was similar, yet different.

Someone had been distilling liquid from this plant, clearly choosing a remote and inaccessible spot to guard against discovery. The making of moonshine was understandable, but what the plant actually was or its use was harder to figure. In its natural state he would probably recognize it, but after being boiled to mush, it was as much a mystery as the rest of the deal.

The still was on his land, though not too far from the border of Triple Cross. Whether that had any significance, he could not guess. None of it seemed to make sense. Still, he had discovered something, something odd enough that whoever had made and operated the distillery was anxious to keep hidden.

Might be worth keeping an eye on it for a while, he thought. After I've had some fishing and get fed up with loafing, I'll maybe swing around and do just that.

Intrigued, though disappointed that he had failed to catch even a glimpse of Cleone, he swung away, penetrating wilder and more remote country. Finally, as the day waned, he came upon a place entirely to his liking. If ever man had been there before, no evidence remained. A small stream slipped past in silence, as though as shy as the wild creatures of these parts. Evergreens stood sentinel at the rim of a meadow.

He unsaddled, then unloaded the pack horse and picketed both animals. Then he suspended most of his pack from a tree branch, beyond the reach of curious or hungry prowlers. He gathered a supply of dry wood, and fished for trout in a pool of the creek. He mixed biscuits, baking them in an improvised Dutch oven, fried the fish and boiled coffee, using some of his fresh supply from town. The drink was as tasty as the meal was satisfying.

A week of this will fix me up as good as new, he reflected contently. The Singer knew what he was talking about: still waters do restore the soul.

Spruce boughs served as mattress beneath his blanket. The last embers of the cookfire winked out. High stars were overhead.

Some sound, alien to the ears even if not to the night, jerked McKay awake. Striving to adjust to the eerie quality of the darkness, he lay motionless, nerves as taut as the strings of a newly tuned banjo, muscles drawn. Whatever had roused him had stirred primeval senses, a heritage from lost days when, a dweller of caves, man had shivered at the roar of the mammoth or the snarl of the saber-toothed tiger.

Now the night was still. The faintly rustling leaves of the big cottonwood under which he had spread his blanket came in muted whisperings. So faint a breeze usually heralded the dawn, but that it was still night seemed confirmed by the opaque blackness his wide-open eyes searched.

There was a thrusting quality to the surrounding

night, a darkness all-pervading, pressing in upon him. Clear sky and a spatter of stars had been visible through the branches overhead when he had dropped off to sleep. At sunset the sky had blazed with fiery splendor across the west, promising a fine day to follow.

Now he could find no star nor rind of moon though he could smell the coming dawn. The air was sharp with frost, as the elevation here was considerably higher than back at the ranch buildings. Normally the tracery like snow would be visible even in the darkness, but now, nothing.

Such blackness was unusual, almost uncanny. Even the night seemed to hold its breath. The cold prickle of fear coursed his spine.

L 1949193

5

Tense, ready for a repetition of whatever had awakened him, McKay's mind skirted recent events, returning rather glumly to Cleo Connor. Much as he disliked the thought, she was Slash's sister, and presumably they would resolve their problems and work as partners. Which was not likely to make it any easier to get to know her better.

Even if she came to realize or understand Slash's ways, and whether or not she approved, Slash would be determined to run the ranch his own way—using its power to harass his neighbors. There had been plenty of signs that he was doing so even while Longpre lived, with or without the older man's consent.

Only weeks ago, Nettleton's small spread to the north of the Triple Cross had been swept by a mysterious fire. Triple Cross cattle grazed where the new growth sprang green. Another small-time neighbor, Tom Dowling, had been found dead, his body decomposed, gnawed by predators. There had been no sure way to determine how he had died.

But now his holdings, to all intents and purposes, formed a part of the Triple Cross.

It was an unpromising background, and any show of friendship or neighborliness would be interpreted by Slash as weakness. It was like the heavy darkness, which showed no sign of lightening.

The aroma of fish from his evening meal lingered faintly, coupled with the harsher smell of coffee from the blackened pot. But the coffee had been good.

The silence seemed as absolute as the darkness, as though whatever sound had roused him had frightened other creatures of the night to a strained immobility. Such fear suggested the hungry snarl of a big cat, or possibly the growl of a grizzly.

Still the quiet held. It was eerie. Tossing aside his blanket, McKay came to his feet. He brushed fingers across a cheek grown bristly since the previous morning, then felt instinctively for the gun at his hip. He'd bedded down fully clothed, removing only his boots.

The cold butt of the six-shooter was reassuring, even though a gun would be of little use when no target was visible. Suddenly, desperately, he craved the light, squinting up and around for some glimmer, however dim.

Fear, a crawling apprehension, seemed to quicken his heartbeat. Despite the dawn chill his clenched palms were sweaty. Light would be not only welcome, it was increasingly desirable. If some predator was prowling, as every instinct warned, light or fire could be a protection.

Suddenly a horse snorted. It was followed by a short hard thud of hoofs as the cayuse was checked by the picket rope. Had more hints been needed, here was proof. The horses had scented the prowler. Now he caught a faint muskiness, rankly wild. Grizzly!

At least he could put a match to the pile of wood made ready the evening before. Forcing himself to steadiness, McKay found a match. He moved a couple of paces to the right, orienting himself by memory, and bent down, fingers reaching. Long ago he had learned to gather dry sticks and lay them for a quick and easy fire, protected by a scrap of canvas. Such readiness saved a hunt through heavy dew.

His fingers felt the frost on the tarp as he tossed it aside. Using a thumbnail, he scratched the match and applied it, still unseeing, listening with strained attention to the crackle and breath of the blaze as the flames took hold.

A wildly fantastic notion, so incredible that he had refused to entertain it, had assailed him as he lit the match. He had not seen its flame. Now the unwilling conviction strengthened as fire licked at flesh. Snatching back his hand he felt increasing heat, and smoke stung his nostrils.

But he hadn't seen the flare of the match, nor could he make out any crimson glow from the crackling flames.

Part of an incomprehensible truth was forced upon him. Such complete and overwhelming blackness was no natural phenomenon, nor had it anything to do with the night. This was terrifying, even as it was inexplicable.

He was blind.

6

Rarely had Slash Connor been faced with a problem that, to his easy egotism, was too complex for ready handling. There were guns or fists or fire for direct action; hidden guns or hired thugs if deceit seemed called for.

Unlike some of his methods, his goals had always been simple and direct. Once he became master of Triple Cross, he aimed to enlarge his holdings by taking over those of his neighbors.

Dowling and Nettleton had served as tests for his theories. Small but satisfactory results could be multiplied.

What he had not counted on was a woman whose claim to the ranch outranked his own and who was also supposed to be his sister. That, along with his growing interest in her, created a complex situation.

"Sounds like we're partners as well as relatives," he acknowledged, liking the first part of the admission. "One of these days, after you've had a chance to rest up and look around, and when I'm not so rushed as right now, we'll go into everything, past and present. But in any case there's no hurry. Seems like the first thing is just to get to know each other."

That was suitable for a temporary partnership, but he realized increasingly that it could be no more than that. Not with such a situation and such a woman.

If she was not his sister, he could marry her, and increasingly he liked the idea. But to confess to her that his father had been a scoundrel, and himself almost equally so, to set their relationship straight and permit a wedding—that would create a totally wrong impression.

Here his ordinarily direct solutions could not be considered. Everything would be decided, of course, should she simply disappear. But that would be too brutal, foreign to the one code he possessed—not to make war on women.

With Cleo, even the thought was repugnant. He liked her. And, he must not forget, his suddenly shaky claims to the ranch could be firmly established only by marrying her. Taken together, it was enough to give a man a headache.

To clamp his jaws and stand unmoving required a strong effort of will, but McKay held himself in check. In the brightening dawn, which he could not detect, he loomed tall, a man who with advancing years would acquire the look of a patriarch. Now the whipcord leanness of a fighter showed, while his open eyes showed pain, staring hungrily but with uncomprehending blankness. This dawn was not for him.

Blindness, he had supposed, was an affliction that came upon people of advancing age or from some particular illness or accident. It was not something to pounce without warning in the dark of the night.

Yet for all the impossibility of such a thing, blind he was. He could feel the heat of the fire; his hand still smarted from it. Smoke was in his nostrils. He thought back wildly to headaches and trifling uncertainties, but he hadn't supposed them to be indicators of any serious trouble. Looking across to the Triple Cross the day before, his vision had been as keen as usual.

As far as he knew, nothing similar had ever happened to any of his ancestors. His mother had used reading glasses in her later years, but his father's sight had remained unimpaired up to his death.

However incredible and for whatever reason, it had happened. Survival, life itself, would depend now on how well he controlled himself, mastering emotions and actions. He must plan and act under conditions as terrifying as they were strange.

He was a long way from his ranch buildings— about as far as it was possible to be while remaining on his own land. Baldy O'Brion, his foreman, knew that he had set off for a few days by himself and that he might be gone for a week or even twice that. Baldy also knew that he was well able to look after himself. So no one would find any early cause to worry.

Three or four weeks hence, if he failed to return, a search would be undertaken, but by then, all sign could easily be lost. In such an interval, storms would wash the land, blotting away all traces. If he was not back long before then, he would never return.

Darting wildly, his mind reverted to the still he had stumbled upon, to the increasingly bad taste of the coffee the cook had served him, but apparently not others of the crew. There might be some connection, though such things seemed too fanciful and widely separated to have any link with this sudden loss of sight. He must think straight and clearly.

Survival was strictly up to himself. Alone on a dark, unfamiliar trail, he could afford no mistakes.

Yet blunders, under such conditions, would be inevitable. A wise man learned by his mistakes.

He could depend on his horse to take him home. Once on its back, he would need only to give it its head. He had chosen a steady animal for this trip, and that was reassuring.

He had picketed both saddle pony and pack animal off in the meadow, but he should be able to hear, and through the sound, to reach them. His stomach reminded him that it was time for breakfast—he was accustomed to starting his day with a hearty meal.

In his pack, suspended in midair from a tree limb, were plenty of supplies, from canned peaches and tomatoes to a slab of bacon.

Experience on other camping trips had refined cooking procedures to a fine art. Dip up water from a creek or spring and fill the coffee pot, place it over the edge of the fire, slice bacon into a pan, add more wood.

But the wood to which he had set fire was already burning down. Getting it lit had seemed a good idea, but that had been his initial miscalculation. There was no chance to find or gather more fuel in time to keep the fire going.

Of course he could eat the bacon raw, along with

leftover biscuits—or he could tighten his belt and go hungry.

The immediate problem, once he reached his horse, would be to locate his saddle and get it on, then head back. Pack and pack saddle could be left behind.

Beyond immediate survival he sensed the loom of other, larger problems. Undoubtedly the big test, the worst part, would come after he was home. He would have to cope with a situation new and unprecedented. New, at least, for him.

The loss of sight was frightening. Whether his blindness could be treated or not, he could only speculate. Sometimes, he remembered hearing, lost vision returned of its own accord, but that was apparently rare, a long chance.

It would be impossible, once he was back, to conceal his disability or hide the extent of disaster. Everyone would know. The word would spread to town, to neighboring ranches—especially to the Triple Cross and Slash Connor.

As Longpre had grown older and Slash more assertive, it had become increasingly certain that an all-out clash, a showdown, was bound to occur.

McKay had been at pains to keep the peace as long as Longpre was at least the nominal boss, hoping for some change for the better, while doubting that any might come. Should trouble erupt, he had felt competent to handle it.

Now he was handicapped, all but helpless. Once

the news reached Slash, he would figure that the time had come to make his move.

But that was in the future—if he managed that far. Now he must get to his horse, get it saddled, and get back to the sprawling lonely mansion he called home.

He tensed at a new sound, close at hand. It was hardly what had wakened him—that must have been louder. But this was almost as ominous, a snuffling that changed to a growl, rising to a raging snarl, then a tearing crunching easy to understand. The prowler was at his supplies, probably on hind feet and rearing high, reaching, ripping open the suspended pack to get at the bacon.

Here he had no need to see. Only a massive grizzly could reach high enough to claw down the pack, suspended well beyond the normal reach of hungry predators.

Simultaneously, frantic plunging sounds from the meadow informed McKay that the horses had again caught scent and perhaps sight of the intruder, and were running until checked by the picket ropes. No sight was needed to understand this.

Bad as would be the loss of his supplies, the panic of the horses was worse. Notoriously nearsighted, prowling the vicinity of the camp and probably with the whiff of meat to egg it on, the grizzly might have failed to see or even scent the animals. But their frantic plunging, along with strong emanations of fear, was attracting its attention. McKay could picture the scene as the grizzly turned to this new diversion.

A louder growl testified to its irritability. Clearly it was in a bad mood, and the continued plunging of the horses was disturbing it. It roared with sudden threat, and McKay heard its plunging rush toward the horses. Already disaster was piling on top of disaster and he was helpless to avert it.

A small but distinct snap testified that a picket rope, or perhaps the sapling to which it had been tied, had broken. Emitting a high squeal of terror, the released cayuse plunged away, the sounds of its hoofs receding. Under the circumstances, that was natural; it was also the worst possible reaction. Had the horse remained quiet, the grizzly would probably have ignored it. Now angered, its predatory instincts roused, it had deserted the pack in hot pursuit of the fleeing horse.

Though he could not be sure, McKay's guess was that the pack horse must be causing most of the disturbance. Old Hammerhead, however frightened, would not take on so. Moreover, a sudden terrified squealing sounded like the pack animal.

The rush of its flight still came back, followed by a high neigh of terror as destruction overtook it.

Knowledge and past experience served in place of vision to tell him what was happening. For a short spurt, no horse could outrun a charging grizzly. Nor could any animal of the North American continent endure the leap of so massive an animal onto its back, coupled with the sweep of mighty paws and tearing jaws.

Sudden silence was eloquent.

By now it must be full daylight, the sun perhaps up, but McKay could detect no change. He was sweating with the certainty of what had happened, the sense of helplessness almost worse than blindness. Ordinarily he would have reacted, taking a hand as a matter of course. To have snatched and used his rifle would have been a gamble, but he would have made the attempt. Now he was in a fresh dilemma.

His pack was ruined, the pack horse killed. But there was still a chance that his saddle pony might be on his picket rope, unnoticed, not molested. That could spell salvation, life itself, if he could reach Hammerhead and get away.

But movement on his part, especially if it was blundering and uncertain, might attract the choleric grizzly, bringing a fresh attack. Yet that had to be risked. For the present, the triumphant bear was probably feasting on his kill, so this would be as good a time as any to make the try.

Moving slowly, feeling about, he found his boots and tugged them on. Orienting himself by his memory of where he had placed fire, now down to embers, with the boughs not far at the side, he moved out. He must have certain articles for the journey that lay ahead, and one was his horse's bridle.

A dozen paces left him sweating afresh. If he headed in the wrong direction to grow more hopelessly confused, he would be in real trouble. Then one foot kicked something that gave a faint jingle, and his fingers found the bridle.

The saddle should be with it, but he could not locate it. Evidently its size and leather had attracted the bear, who, finding it inedible, had tossed things about in a growing anger.

Well, he could manage without a saddle. Hammerhead, still frightened, was breathing heavily, moving uneasily. But the sounds were a beacon, and McKay headed straight though nervously, fearful of stumbling. Reaching the still-picketed cayuse, he soothed him. McKay got the bit into the horse's mouth, untied the picket rope, and swung onto the animal's back with a lift of arms and kick of legs.

It was fortunate that he maintained a tight grip on the reins. Instantly, even with the snub, the cayuse took off. Such speed might disturb the grizzly, but McKay decided that the pony would veer well away. In any case, there was nothing to do now but trust its sagacity and speed.

7

Normally, with a good horse between his legs, McKay felt equal to any occasion, but being forced to travel blindly, while a bad-tempered grizzly was on the prowl, was a nightmare. He was incapable of guiding, and a badly frightened cayuse was as likely to do something wrong as right. But there was no choice.

Giving the horse its head, he tried to relax, aware that his jaws were as tightly clenched as his hands. The lack of a saddle made relaxing more difficult. For the first time the full impact of his personal disaster hit like a blow, bringing a feeling of numbness, increasing the sense of helplessness. Always before in the face of trouble he had been able to fight back. Now there was nothing to hit at, no trail to follow.

If there had been any real warning of what was coming, giving him a chance to plan and adjust, it might be possible to conceal his disability, at least for a while, to carry on without too much disruption. With a few weeks for planning and preparation he could have trained himself to move inside the house, to cross from it to the barn and find the proper stall. Now...

Realizing that his eyes were as tightly shut as his hands, he opened them, but there was no change. For the moment the pony was running easily, at a ground-covering trot, and he set himself to recall, to picture, what until then he had taken for granted. The big, sprawling house, so out of proportion to his own needs, standing for the most part empty.

His memory, sharpened now, was both excellent and accurate. More than once he had prowled the house in the night, using no light, and he could do so again, room by room, upstairs or down. At least the house stood sharp and clear.

Mentally he toured it, then went on to the turn

from the kitchen door, the number of steps to the barn; the turn from the stall to where his saddle hung, bridle beside it, saddle blanket draped across it. Those things he could manage almost by instinct, needing no light. The real rub would be when he got out of the barn. To make a start in the direction he wanted to go would be easy, but how ever to follow across open country or at turns in the trail?

Time to study and plan might have helped, but now the transition was as total as it had been sudden. He was lost, almost helpless.

Again he forced back panic, the impulse to kick his horse into a wild run, to strike out in blind retaliation. Whatever came, he had to hold himself in check. Giving in to panic would finish him.

He would have to trust to others, and that was the worst part. Who, under these circumstances, could he trust, literally with his life? Certainly not Baldy O'Brion, who had been his foreman for the past three years. Baldy knew cattle and possessed a natural capacity for taking charge, excellent qualities for a man in his position.

As long as he knew that he was watched, he would do a good job.

That had been more or less understood between them. McKay managed his ranch, and very little that went on escaped him. Or so it had been. Now it would be a changed situation, and he couldn't depend on O'Brion. Baldy would take advantage, not from any lack of loyalty—McKay had learned that with him it was a nonexistent quality—but simply with an eye to feathering his own nest. A blind man was bound to be a loser, and Baldy would not want to be on the losing side.

As for the others of his crew, one by one he reviewed them, what they would think, how they would react. Each was predictable. Some he could trust, men such as Folger and Jim O'Donnell. All were good hands for the jobs they had to do.

That about summed it up. Tell them what to do, and they required no further direction. But he doubted if any had the ability or initiative to take O'Brion's place, or actually his own, as was now required.

His thoughts went on to Rawhide. Once the name had been as accurate as it was symbolic. Gradually the town was changing, mellowing. Its citizens were no longer braced for trouble, nor did they expect it. With someone like Slash Connor moving recklessly toward a goal, most of them would draw back in dismay.

He had plenty of acquaintances there, even a few friends. McKay mulled the list. Doc Slingsby—Old Doc, graying like a badger, but just as peppery. He would have to visit Doc as soon as possible, have him look him over and render an opinion, do what he could. But it was unlikely that the doctor could be of much help in this sudden affliction. Such blindness would be as far outside Slingsby's experience as his own. Old Doc was competent, maybe better than average in his profession, but there were limits.

His mind ranged on to Phineas Chadwin, attorney at law, the only lawyer within a radius of a hundred miules. Almost certainly, in this new crisis, he would have need of legal advice. In such a case he could trust Chadwin no further than Baldy O'Brion.

And so it went. The banker, Andrew Kirk— perhaps. A man of rectitude and a certain ability. But running a small-town bank was about the measure of his capabilities.

Ordinarily, when there was something to do, McKay knew where to find help, how to direct men, to supervise them. The trouble now was his inability to watch, to really supervise.

Hammerhead continued at a trot, proof that he was heading for his accustomed stable and anxious to get there. The encounter with the grizzly was unsettling, and the barn loomed as refuge. He could be depended on to find his way back.

Certainly by now the bear had been left well behind. McKay was lucky to that extent, though two such pieces of bad luck at the same time, blindness and the prowling silvertip, combined for a grim coincidence.

The sun was in his face, proof that it was full day and warming, even though he could catch no glimpse of light. Whatever had hit him would rate as unusual. The flesh was heir to a vast number of afflictions, even if the average person never suffered many of them.

That again was the frightening part. With something known, more or less normal, there would be hope of treatment and possible cure. But with a rare, little-understood blindness, the odds against help were sharply increased.

Sweating again, he battled panic, almost maddened at the prospect of such endless night, of his helplessness. Then he shook himself. There was one good aspect. He had a fight on his hands, to hold on to his ranch, to build a new life out of wreckage. And he had always enjoyed a good fight.

The liquid-sweet notes of a meadowlark drifted from overhead. McKay's throat tightened. At least his hearing was unimpaired. His remaining senses would sharpen in an effort to compensate for the loss of vision.

The trouble was that nothing ever could.

He flinched and dodged in sudden pain as something slapped his face. At the same moment he realized that his cayuse was pushing through a tangle of brush, perhaps trees, probably taking the most direct route since there was no road or trail and his rider was leaving the route up to him. McKay clenched his jaws and threw up a warding hand, freshly aware of his helplessness. There could be very real danger—

There was. A heavy, clublike impact rammed his forehead. The next instant he was on the ground, dazed, knocked clear off the horse. Reason suggested that it had been a low, outstretched tree limb under which Hammerhead was gone easily enough, but he had had no warning, no chance to dodge.

The earth seemed to spin wildly. He dug his fingers into the ground to steady himself. Dizziness was another side-effect of blindness, producing reactions both new and unpredictable.

His fingers found a thick growth of plants, not grass as he had first supposed, not brush or shrub, but some type of weed. The scent from the plants sharpened another sense, and he tested it with his nose, remembering from past experience, identifying the smell. Locoweed.

As a cattleman, he was familiar with two or three species of loco, which grew at scattered intervals across the ranch. Usually the weed was sparse, but now and again it flourished in dense clumps or patches, as seemed to be the case here. Innocent enough in appearance, innocuous-seeming on hillside or meadow, loco could assume a deadly potency. Horses or cattle usually avoided it when grazing, but when they acquired a taste for it, they would seek out the weed like a drunkard craving more and more liquor.

McKay had seen the effects among his own stock. A mild addiction could give a horse or cow the blind staggers, send it running crazily, or cause it to stand dumbly, starving in the midst of plenty. Eating it led to all manner of locoed behavior, from which the plant derived its name. In the end, unless the animals were removed to fresh pasture, shut away from the poison they had come to crave, it could lead to death.

Normally, due to its wide dispersion and the instinct of an animal to avoid it, loco was not much of a problem. But he had fallen into a patch. McKay's sense of smell, doubly acute as his eyes refused their office, fitted memories into place.

The odor was familiar. Here was the smell that had clung about the remote and hidden still he had stumbled upon—altered, but not to be mistaken.

And it was the same smell, barely reaching the nose but lodged mostly in taste, that had been in his morning coffee these last several weeks, spoiling it for him. He realized now that it was not a pot in need of scouring, but its contents—the distilled essence of locoweed had been added to the brew, a slow-acting but potent poison!

8

Cleone Connor was a literal-minded person, inclined to directness in thought and action. The sudden loss of her mother, with its attendant revelations, had dismayed but not frightened her. She took the prospect of a long, hard journey, unaccompanied, to a new country and unknown relatives almost as a challenge. Since it had to be done, she would do it.

At Triple Cross, she was still dismayed but not quite frightened. There was something wrong, but it was intangible, not something she could see or understand. Slash—he had stared in blank, uncomprehending astonishment when she had called him Ashley—was courteous, even considerate, but evasive and unapproachable. She could not talk things over, pin him down, come to grips with the situation.

It was as though she was merely a guest, not unwelcome but hardly wanted, rather than a sister, at least half-owner of this big, remote ranch. Something was wrong, and her inability to get to the truth was what bothered her.

Well, she could saddle a horse and ride. That was always pleasant, and here it would be useful, revealing. And there was the possibility—she colored faintly and refused to acknowledge the hope—that she might catch a glimpse of their neighbor, perhaps even exchange greetings with David McKay. He had proved himself a good neighbor, a gentleman, and he might be a friend.

She sensed increasingly that she might need a friend.

McKay's mind, briefly dazed from the smash of the limb, was all at once as keen as ever. Here, he sensed, might be the answer to the bad taste of the coffee, to the headaches and increasing discomfort that had afflicted him. Like a horse, he was locoed.

Cause and effect could hardly be coincidence. 'Lias Shaney was a good cook, a couple of cuts above the usual hash-slinger who traveled with a chuck wagon or occupied a kitchen. In moments when he had resorted to the comfort of a bottle he liked to boast that he had cooked in town restaurants, besides having served an apprenticeship to a pharmacist in a drugstore while little more than a boy.

From such a background, particularly the pharmacy, he would have at least a smattering of knowledge. It might be inadequate, but he could easily have picked up the knack of constructing and operating a still to extract juices in place of whiskey; and he would probably know something of the potential of distillates from so deadly a weed.

Much was becoming clear. Shaney, unquestionably bribed by someone, had made the still, gathered the loco and obtained its essence, and was gradually poisoning him. Shaney was the sort who would regard that with an almost scientific detachment, interested to observe the results. Probably he hadn't figured that it might cause blindness, either temporary or permanent. If the loco incapacitated his employer to an increasing extent—well, undoubtedly that was the desired result.

Should it kill him, who could ever know or even suspect the bizarre nature of his affliction? And Shaney's other employer could disclaim any suspicion of guilt or knowledge.

Perhaps he was wrong, but it seemed to McKay that he had stumbled on the answer. Hopefully in time to reverse the illness, though perhaps too late ever to see again. Horses and cattle went blind if they ate enough loco, and usually, once that state was reached, they died.

He sat up, feeling of his head, still shaky from the fall. A touch of blood on his fingers was warm and sticky, while a throbbing ache attested to the severity of the blow. Scrambling to his feet, he reeled dizzily, but managed a hoarse call to his horse, too late to be of any use. Panic drove out the dizziness, and he started on a blind run but checked himself. That could only make matters worse.

There was no response to his shout, no sound. He forced himself to consider, for it was unlikely that, with reins loose and hampering, the pony would go far. He was too well trained for that, but he had probably gone ahead a number of steps. Without a snort or whinney or at least the jingle of bridle, McKay was helpless to find him.

He called without much hope of any response. The closer the pony might be, the more he would expect McKay to walk up and remount.

A couple of steps, with arms outstretched, brought him to a tree. There would be a scatter of them, along with brush. His horse was probably grazing, working toward more open ground.

That brought a sharper remembrance of his own hunger, the missed breakfast despite his careful plans of the previous evening. Unlike Hammerhead, he could do nothing about it. But at least there was nothing to lose by moving on. The trees seemed to be thinning, and he called again, wondering whether he should fire a few shots as a signal. It was only remotely possible that anyone would be within hearing.

He was sweating, feeling the increasing warmth of the sun, but it was the helplessness, an abyss even blacker than his blindness, that really bothered him, goading like madness. Never, even in the first moments of realization, had he been so tested.

Without his horse he was stranded deep in the heart of a wilderness. The chances that he might be found, at least in time, were so slender that a gambler would refuse such odds. To come upon water again was equally unlikely, but thirst would increase with the heat of the day. Once more he shouted, aware that the sound came out more like a yell, high with desperation.

An answer, from quite close at hand, left him numbed with disbelief. Groping in endless night, he had expected nothing, not really hoping. Moreover, it was a woman's voice, and if men were a rarity hereabouts, a woman was ten times more unusual.

Still, the voice was a partial explanation. It belonged to Cleo Connor.

His hearing, more acute than usual, informed him that a horse was approaching. Of course she would have been out for a ride. Chance or luck had led her this way. She would not have known or cared that she had strayed well across the border between the two ranches.

"Is something wrong, Mr. McKay?" she asked, and he was struck anew by the soft yet vital quality of her voice.

McKay hesitated, faced with an admission that, like the blindness itself, might alter his whole life. But since it had to be made, better to her than any other. He felt sure of her sympathy.

"Wrong enough, Miss Cleone. I'm lost. You see—or rather, the trouble is that I can't see. During the night I lost my sight. I've gone blind."

He elaborated where normally the statement alone would have been enough, but it was still too new, too incredible for an easy explanation.

"Blind? You!" She sounded as startled as shocked. "But how—I don't understand—"

"Neither do I," he confessed ruefully, but the double blackness of despondency was lifting. The relief at being found where there had been only a faint hope for discovery was a strong antidote to discouragement. And that the one who had found him was Cleo, who was increasingly in his thoughts—and, he knew now, in his heart—somehow that seemed as sure as destiny.

"I know that it seems crazy, impossible," he added carefully. "I was all right when I went to sleep last night. But today I can't see a thing, not even a gleam of light. I got on my horse, figuring that he'd head for home, and I suppose he was taking a pretty straight course. But he ran under the low branch of a tree and knocked me off—"

Relief, after the tenseness of the last hours, was like opening a floodgate, but he put a curb on his emotions. He could not breathe a word, least of all to her, of his suspicions and conclusions about who might have bribed his cook to such a betrayal. No one would go to such lengths without strong motives.

But whatever he thought, he had no proof. In any case, Cleo was new to this country, ignorant of the dark undercurrents that ravaged the range. She was guiltless of any complicity, even if Slash was her brother. But was he? McKay still had his doubts.

9

He sensed that she had dismounted and was close beside him. The tide of sympathy that flowed from her was as real as in the tone of her voice.

"Why this—this is terrible, David. So awful—"

She checked, as if sensing how her own emotions had surprised her into the intimate use of his name. "But at least your horse is only a short way off," she hurried on. "But I—I can't understand how you could lose your sight so suddenly, in such fashion—"

"I don't understand it either," McKay admitted. "It's left me in the dark in more ways than one. And after I was brushed off my horse and knew how totally lost and helpless I was, I was never so glad to see—at least to hear—anyone, in all my life."

"You poor man! I can see—understand, how you must feel! I'll catch your horse now, before it strays any farther. I'll be right back," she added reassuringly, strongly aware of how he must feel. Presently she was back, placing the reins in his hands.

"Can you ride all right? I'll go with you to make sure that you get back home without any more trouble. It's my turn, anyway, to see you home," she added, with an attempt at lightness.

Hunger was relegated to a minor discomfort in his overpowering relief. He remounted and sensed her closeness as she rode alongside, while Hammerhead set off as though nothing had happened.

If she was curious about where he had been or the events leading up to his mishap, she asked no questions. Then, as the silence lengthened, she ventured a remark.

"Isn't this a beautiful day! Oh—I'm sorry."

"Because I can't see it? At least I can feel the sun,

and with you, it's turning into almost a wonderful day." There was a calming effect in her companionship, a steadying reassurance. "Now my luck's not all bad, what with you coming along."

"I'm glad I did, though I suppose it was one chance in a thousand that I happened to ride far enough and in the right direction. But how did you manage at first? You don't have a saddle—"

Gradually she drew from him what had happened, including the ill-tempered grizzly and its attack on his pack horse. That she sensed the terror of his ordeal was vibrant in her voice, but with fuller understanding her sympathy took a practical turn.

"So you missed your breakfast and must be half starved! I've no bacon or biscuits, but would you settle for a roasted trout? There's a creek just ahead, and I have a fish line and hooks. When I started out, I thought I might catch my dinner, with a willow for a pole."

"Trout sounds wonderful. Next to seeing again—to seeing so lovely a lady—I can't think of anything I'd like better."

"Then we won't waste of time. Here is the creek. If you want a drink—" She took his hand as he dismounted, then hesitated. "The water's so near but so far..."

"I'll stretch out and drink," he said. The coolness of the water was like nectar. Sitting up, his senses more than normally acute, he heard the gurgle of a deep pool, then Cleo's excited exclamation as she tossed out a hook baited with a grasshopper and had it almost instantly taken. Clearly the trout's hunger matched his own.

Within minutes she was back, her voice breathless from excitement.

"I've never seen such fishing—and I love to fish! I've half a dozen big ones!"

He could almost follow her preparations by her deliberate stream of talk while she found dry wood amid the brush that fringed the creek and built a fire. Clearly she was no stranger to such cookery. She rolled the cleaned fish in leaves stripped from some plant that grew at the water's edge and roasted them in the coals. The aroma was tantalizing.

"I'm sorry that there are no biscuits or coffee," she said. "If I'd known that it could turn into a picnic, I'd have raided the kitchen for supplies. But I did bring salt."

She placed a fish, hot from the roasting, on a plate-sized leaf and into his hands.

"Can you manage, or shall I help?" she asked, and was reassured by his sudden laugh.

"I'll do fine from here. Watch me." He had no trouble stripping the crisp flesh from the long ridge bone. She leaned to sprinkle it with salt, her shoulder and hand touching him, her breath soft against his cheek. He guessed that she had been equally hungry.

"I had my breakfast, but somehow I'm ravenous! I can almost sympathize with that bear!"

Presently they went on, the companionship and a full stomach partly offsetting McKay's dismay at his lack of orientation. Normally he could find his way without much trouble, even in strange country and in storm or darkness, but now he had no idea of where they were, no point from which to start. Cleo talked determinedly of other matters, far afield from the immediate reality. Sensing her purpose, he responded in similar vein.

He had come a long way the day before, adding miles by a roundabout course. Apparently she had a good sense of direction and knew where Lost Horse Ranch and its buildings lay.

Save for pauses to drink as they crossed creeks, they did not stop as the day wore on. Several more hours would be required to get back, and he began to wonder increasingly about Cleo.

"I'm afraid this is spoiling your plans, taking you so far out of your way."

"I had no particular plan, except for a ride and a trout dinner," she returned serenely. "I've had both. And I'm glad that I can return the favor, that I can help, even a little."

If she had perhaps entertained any doubts as to the realness of his affliction, they had been dispersed. From the slant of sun, he could tell that day was drawing toward evening.

The steady beat of trotting hoofs told them that someone was coming. Cleo's voice was slightly breathless.

"Someone is coming—one of your men, I'm sure, Mr. McKay. And I can see your buildings in the distance. So I'll leave you here, to get back. I hope things will work out for you—as well as possible. Good-bye."

He sensed that she was anxious to be gone, but a hail from the other rider spoiled her plan. He recognized the tones of Baldy O'Brion.

"Hi, Boss." Despite long association, and O'Brion's awareness that he did not much like it, Baldy generally called him Boss rather than using his name. "Looks like you found company. No wonder you headed back sooner'n you'd planned! Reckon I'd have done the same."

Cleo gave him a civil greeting, then was gone, as the receding hoofbeats testified. The foreman was clearly bewildered.

"Now what's wrong?" he wondered. "She's a strange lady, but a mighty pretty one. I ain't that poison, am I? Or did it sort of upset her to have your little secret spoiled? Oh, now I get it. Reckon she must be Slash Connor's sister, who's just out from the east."

"She is."

"Ain't you the sly dog! Who'd have figured you'd even have met her, let alone getting to know her so well?"

"I gave her a ride out from town to the Triple Cross the other day." McKay was tired and suddenly irritable. "Today she found me, when I was lost and afoot, and returned the favor by making sure that I got back all right."

"Lost? Afoot?" O'Brion apparently noticed his condition for the first time, noting the lack of a saddle as well as the missing pack horse and the other signs that things had not gone well. "You look like you'd had trouble. What on earth happened?"

"Plenty. Let's get on to the house. I'm tired."

"Sure, sure, Boss. But from the looks of you, you might have been scrappin' a bear or something—"

"It was the next thing to that. A grizzly messed up my camp this morning, and chased and killed my pack horse."

Baldy whistled, waiting for an elaboration. When it did not follow, he probed obliquely.

"Toby was tellin' me, just last night, about findin' a dead cow, partly eaten, way off to the west, beyond Hunter's Springs. He thought it looked like the work of a grizzly."

"More than likely it was the same animal.

Chances are he's been wounded or trapped—hurt just enough to turn him into a marauder, with an old wound aching and making him savage."

"Sounds reasonable. And he hit your camp? Why, you've even lost your saddle and rifle!"

"That part wasn't the bear's fault, at least not directly. Or the reason why I needed a guide to make it back here. I'm blind."

"Blind?" Baldy repeated, his astonishment tinged with disbelief. "You mean that you—you can't see?"

"Not a thing." Since the story had to be told, it might as well be now. "That's why the bear was able to get away with so much. Otherwise I'd at least have tried a shot at him."

He supplied some details, which O'Brion seemed to find hard to believe. McKay could hardly blame him. Once convinced, O'Brion's remark was cryptic yet characteristic.

"Blind—and lost if the lady hadn't just happened along to help out! What a hell of a piece of luck! But you blind! Now ain't that the devil of a thing!"

10

Shaney was sympathetic and solicitous, perhaps no more than such developments called for, but McKay, listening with a suddenly acute understanding, detected both triumph and excitement in his tones. Big Mac's impulse was to fire the cook— not merely that, but to throw him out bodily—but he resisted the temptation. He had a small revenge when Shaney announced that his supper was on the table, a substantial meal to make up for what he had missed during the day.

"Steak and spuds, with plenty of gravy, hot biscuits and coffee. Good hot coffee, just the way you like it."

"I'll eat with the boys tonight," McKay said, and made his way across the yard without veering, leaving Shaney speechless for once. A surprised, uneasy silence descended on the crew as he took his former place at the table.

"Nothing like company when you're in the dark," he observed. "I'll have to trouble you to fill my plate along with yours, Jim," he added to Jim O'Donnell at his left. "Likely I'll be clumsy, not very good table manners, but I'll manage."

They could not guess how much of an ordeal it was, but he had to go on living, not withdraw into a shell. It was an effort to make each move slow and deliberate, but the restraint helped. Getting food on to his fork was the hardest; finding his mouth was simpler. Becoming aware of the continuing silence, he paused.

"You boys go on talking," he admonished. "This isn't the end of the world. Tomorrow I'll go to town and see Doc Slingsby. And between all of us, we'll make out to keep the old horse kicking."

At the close of the meal most lingered to express their sympathy, to assure him, somewhat uncertainly, that they would help in every way possible. Since he was sure that most of them meant it, it was reassuring. But finding his way around a no longer quite familiar house, always overlarge and now huge, locating bed and chair and sitting down, was almost as bad as the first sudden realization at dawn that catastrophe had struck without warning.

But the day had not been all bad. Some of his luck had been good, and more than good.

One of his first tasks would have to be going from room to room, floor to floor, through the entire house, until the floor plans were fixed in his memory like instinct. It would be the best sort of training, and he had to gain a sure, easy familiarity of movement.

He was too tired to lie awake that night. Dressing the next morning was almost routine. He considered shaving but decided against the attempt. If he didn't cut his throat, he would botch the job. A straight-edge was too sharp for even memory and touch. It would be simpler to visit a barber when he reached town.

O'Donnell drove, a fast-stepping team hitched to the buggy. They covered the score of miles in record time, with McKay's other sharpened senses informing him of their progress. Twice they splashed through Lost Horse Creek, the iron-shod wheels grating on the rocky bottom. At the halfway mark he caught the shrill barking of prairie dogs where the road skirted a considerable town of the scurrying rodents. The sharp pungency of alkali assailed the nostrils as dust arose across a whitish strip near the town.

Walking down the street, after they had left the buggy, his fingers lightly on O'Donnell's arm, he was aware how other sounds faded to sudden hush. He recognized two or three voices. He waited instinctively for the usual familiar hail and greeting; words that did not come.

His mouth drew to a tight line. It was not the lack of salutations that bothered him, since friends as well as acquaintances might find themselves suddenly tongue-tied, uncertain of what to say or whether to speak at all. The bodeful aspect of such silence was that it should happen, sure proof that virtually everyone had already heard the news.

Reports of his blindness and helplessness had run ahead like smoke shoved by a strong wind. In that lay not only a hint of trouble but the breath of treachery.

He should have been ahead of such news, instead of the other way around. Someone from his own crew had wasted no time in spreading the report.

Red Hughson, whose tongue usually outran the snip of his shears, shaved him in silence. It was only as McKay stood up from the chair that the shop door banged and a voice exclaimed heartily:

"What's all this talk about you, Dave? I just hit town and heard the story. It's unbelievable."

A strong but calloused hand closed on his own. McKay warmed to the clasp. Frank Brewer was a neighbor on the opposite boundary from Triple Cross, and he was demonstrating a proven friendship.

"No tellin' what they're saying about me." McKay managed a grin. "And whatever it is, I probably deserve it."

"It's true, then—you can't see?"

"Not even a shadow, Frank."

He could envision Brewer's bewildered head-shake, but the clasping fingers grew firmer.

"Now ain't that a hell of a thing! I never heard of such a thing. But knowing you, Dave, I'm sure of one thing. You'll lick it."

Such friendship was heartening. Since O'Donnell had left to do some shopping, Brewer escorted him to the doctor's office. Slingsby's grunt as he took McKay's arm and led him to a window, peering silently into wide-open eyes, was assurance that he too had heard the story. There was the scratch of a match, the pungency as the brief flame was held near his nose as an additional test. He did not blink. Slingsby exhaled in a long *whoosh,* steered him to a chair, then sank creakingly into his own.

"Tell me about this, just the way it happened, Dave," he instructed.

"There's not much to tell," McKay returned. It would be better not to voice suspicions that he had no way of proving, at least not now. He gave an account of his awakening to double disaster, elaborating as Slingsby prodded with questions. As he finished, the silence grew prolonged.

"Your eyes hadn't been troublin' you any before that? Nothing but for a few headaches?"

"Nothing that I remember."

He could sense Old Doc's baffled headshake.

"This is mighty unusual. I've heard of similar cases, of course, of folks losing their sight kind of sudden. But I've never seen or known anything of the sort."

"Meaning there's nothing you can do?"

"That's about the size of it. I'm no eye doctor to start with, of course. You could see a specialist— have to go to some big city though."

"What good would that do? Could a specialist operate?"

"What could he operate for? If you'd been losing sight for a long while, going gradually blind, then it'd most likely be cataracts. Some doctors do operate in such cases. Guess it's kind of a tricky thing, but they do these days. But in your case..."

He left the words hanging, his meaning clear. McKay had been pretty sure from the first. This was a strange, rare affliction, and there was nothing that could be done. Slingsby tried to offer some comfort.

"This coming on the way it did, there's a chance—maybe not a very big one, but still a possibility—that you'll be able to see again, someday. I can't explain how or why, but nature is the best healer."

Probably he didn't really believe that, but he was a friend and kindly. Hard sense assured McKay that even if anything of the sort should happen, it was unlikely to come soon enough to do much good. Given time, he could more or less adjust to the situation, and matters might work out. But the showdown would come soon. He was convinced that he had been fed an extract of loco for just such a purpose, and the situation was ripe and would be followed up. Unless he could meet the challenges that would be offered, he would lose his ranch, perhaps even his life. Which, if it came to that, might be the best solution.

But he was of no mind to submit tamely. The problem was how to fight against increasing odds. The silences of most men whom he had counted as friends was assurance that they would not prove allies; he could count on few besides himself.

His thoughts reverted to Cleo. She had almost certainly saved his life. The ironic part was that she should be sister to the man who would grab eagerly at the chance to get his ranch away from him, and who, beyond much doubt, was behind this whole scheme. Her position was likely to be as difficult as his own, or even worse, caught in the middle of a mess not of her making or to her liking.

The distillation of loco must have affected his sight, just as eating the weed could blind horses or cattle. It might have been administered to him over a longer period than he had suspected. Whether the effects would be temporary or permanent he could only wait to learn. He was pretty much on his own—and very much in the dark, in every sense.

Home again, he made certain changes. The first was to discharge Shaney. He installed Toby in his place, despite O'Brion's bewildered protest.

"But why? Shaney's a good hasher. Reckon he knows more about it than most anybody—all the ins and outs of food an' drink, as you might say."

"Could be he does. That could be the trouble. He's fired."

"You mean you ain't even keepin' him on as a regular hand?"

"I want him off Lost Horse, a long way off. Today."

From O'Brion's mutterings, it was clear that he thought more than the boss's eyesight was affected. If the men thought his mental faculties were affected, it might increase his difficulties, but there was no help for that. Even if he should tell what he suspected, it would only convince others that he really was loco.

There was bright sunshine. McKay could tell that by standing in the open, feeling its warmth. Abruptly he turned back inside, closing the door, but he could not shut out the agony of knowing it was there and, like all the world beyond, barred by invisible walls. Bitterness rose like heartburn.

He swung at a knock, a sharp, peremptory rap at the door. His voice betrayed none of the despair seething inside.

"Come in."

Someone pushed through, then remained standing, looking him over. In the silence was a mocking quality.

"Well?" McKay demanded.

"So you're blind, McKay. Tough luck."

Almost by instinct he had known who this visitor would be. Slash Connor had wasted little time once the news had reached him. That he had

long been unwelcome on Lost Horse land was a
fact he chose to disregard.

McKay could picture him, increasingly fleshy in
this last year from overindulgence in the liquor
that had been his father's downfall, but not yet
flabby; arrogant, impatient of delay. That he had
long eyed the neighboring spread covetously was
no secret.

"A tough break," Slash went on softly. "I've
been trying to picture it, and it's difficult. Your
shirt's buttoned wrong," he added with calculated
mockery.

He might be telling the truth and probably was.
McKay's fingers had been clumsy that morning, a
sense of futility overriding all else. But the
mockery was a tonic. Anger could be a powerful
restorative.

"You didn't come over to console me over my
hard luck," he returned flatly.

"Well, no, I didn't. I came on business." Connor
saw no need for beating about the bush. This
blindness was better than he had expected, and in
his philosophy, the time to crowd your luck was
when it was running strong. "I came to talk
business. Your being blind changes everything.
You won't be able to handle such an outfit, not
even with good help. I'll buy you out."

Connor had considered his own aspect, the
problems involved should McKay accept his offer.
The rub would come in raising the money. Then he

had been reassured. Land poor he might be, but the two outfits combined as one represented a lot of wealth, both real and potential. He would be able to get the necessary loan.

"What makes you think I'd want to sell?"

"You know you can't run the ranch. You're as good as helpless. I'll give you ten thousand—cash, for land and cattle."

His bluntness matched the brashness of the offer. His manner showed his certainty that McKay had no choice. No one would back a blind man. No one would be so foolish or reckless as to contest with Slash Connor for its purchase, knowing that, even if they were successful in winning the property, they would have him and his bitter animosity on their border. He was in the saddle, and his way was to ride roughshod.

"Ten thousand?" McKay repeated. Incredulity checked him momentarily. He had expected more taunting, but this offer, far below the real value, was sheer robbery. His fingers worked. One thing was in his favor—he had been sightless only a couple of days, but with ever-sharpening senses, he could tell where Connor stood, his precise position in the room.

"Get out," McKay ordered thickly. "Get out and off my land! And stay off!"

Slash's laughter was mocking, a taunt and dare.

"Yeah? Who's going to make me?"

11

Slash Connor was sure of himself, completely certain. For a while he had prudently discounted reports, suspecting some kind of trick, but now it was clear that he had to deal with a blind man. So this was the time to push his luck, to grab the neighboring spread he had desired for as long as he could remember. But to all that, a new and potent quality had been added.

Cleone. Until now no woman had counted in his scheme of things, but her coming had changed everything. She had a strained, unreal relationship both to himself and to the ranch. And though he called it his own, actually it was hers; and for that, she was desirable and must be his. Not only as the key to the ranch, but on her own account.

But, riding across to Lost Horse, he had come face to face with a blank wall. As a cowboy had once remarked, wantin' and gettin' is two different things.

It was a tangled situation, and he could discover no solution. Now there was one factor on which to fix his fury, his sudden wild jealousy of this man who stood before him. Chance had thrown the two of them together, Cleo riding out from town with McKay, then coming upon him when he most needed help. That she had given it quickened his apprehension even as it spurred his jealousy.

"Who's going to stop me?" he repeated. The solution to his problems was suddenly simple. Get rid of this man, and nothing could stand in his way.

A matching rage was in McKay. Too long he had been forced to creep instead of walk, to be led instead of leading. Here was a chance to hit back, to come to grips with the man he was now certain was behind all his troubles.

"I am," he returned, and moved with a speed matched only by its sureness.

His senses did not deceive him. Big hands reaching, arms outspread, he was upon Connor, closing, grappling with an iron intensity before the startled man from Triple Cross could comprehend or counter. Part was luck, obtaining the hold he wanted, pinning Slash's arms to his sides so that his frantic struggles were as useless as those of a roped calf. Elation was a wild elixir. Through hours growing to days McKay had held himself in an iron control, with life suddenly out of reach along a darkened trail.

Now he had Connor in his grasp, a chance to answer in kind. A man could ask no more.

Slash was caught completely off guard. Even with their eyes open, men had learned better than to tangle with him. For some time it had been his unanswered boast that he could lick anyone foolish or foolhardy enough to contest with him.

That McKay, impotent in darkness, would even think of trying had not occurred to him.

He struggled frantically, bewildered to find himself helpless in a grip becoming ever more relentless. They strained together, boots rasping, exhaling in sudden gasps, deadly silent. All at once, gathering his strength, McKay lifted, sensing the change as Connor's feet left the floor. He held him poised for an instant, then, exerting the pent-up violence of the hours of frustration, threw him, hurtling like a sack of wheat, toward the open door.

A splintering crash told McKay that somewhere he had miscaluclated. Clearly his senses had not readjusted with full accuracy to his altered situation. He had felt a soft wind through the open door and had intended to throw Connor out through it. Somehow he had missed the door, tossing Slash instead through the window, as the shattering tinkle of glass coupled with crashing frame made clear.

Mentally he shrugged. The loss of a window was a small price to pay for the satisfaction of tossing his enemy through it. And blind though he was, he was still master in his own house, still a man to be reckoned with, not mocked.

And there was a second satisfaction. That most of Slash Connor's boasting of physical invincibility had been directed, not too subtly, against him had become more and more apparent. Many people had accepted it, believing that even Dave McKay shied away from battling with so dread a neighbor.

Then the triumph faded, the sense of entrapment and helplessness flooding back. McKay tensed at the sounds outside. Clearly Slash had not only survived so violent an exit, but was stirring, and McKay could only guess at what his next move might be. Maddened by humiliation, Slash's reactions at such times were akin to those of a coiled rattler striking out in blind fury.

If he came back through the door with his gun blazing, he would have things all his own way. There would be no chance to get hold of him again, no time to dodge, no time for retreat.

McKay raised a hand to his face, wiping away sweat. His mind reverted, with sudden understanding and sympathy, to a trapped coyote— helpless to run or resist, awaiting the bitter end of a bullet, hating most of all so ignominious an ending. When man or animal could no longer fight...

Jim O'Donnell's voice, coming from somewhere beyond the door, broke the paralysis of silence, and McKay relaxed. He had supposed himself alone at the cluster of buildings because Slash Connor had been able to walk in on him unchallenged. The crew were scattered to the far parts of the range. Even Toby, who would ordinarily have been struggling with his new duties as hasher, had set out for town to lay in more supplies.

"I don't think I'd do that, Connor—not if I was you." O'Donnell had lost his drawl, sudden sharpness in his tone. "Shooting a blind man would rate as murder!"

Clearly his guess had been accurate. An inarticulate snarl was Connor's response as he turned away, boots stomping with frustration. Within moments came the receding beat of a horse's hoofs.

McKay sucked in a deep breath, picturing the scene. Slash was probably cut and bruised from his violent departure through the window. His reaction, grabbing for his gun, had been predictable.

But the lady called luck had lent another whimsical twist to a deadly situation, as O'Donnell had happened along in time to witness Connor's exit via the window and his murderous intent. Probably he had enforced his suggestion with his own gun at the ready. At least a witness, coupled with the warning that shooting a blind man would rate as murder, had checked Slash.

A step at the door signaled O'Donnell. His mildly humorous drawl held a thread of amazed respect.

"Kind of wasteful of window glass, ain't you, Dave? The way he come bustin' through it, he sure didn't leave much."

"He sort of riled me," McKay explained. "Said he came over to buy me out, then made out like I had to take his offer, whether I liked it or not. Ten thousand."

O'Donnell whistled. "The stingy offspring of a poison pup! That's almost a bigger insult than a pair of two-bit pieces!"

"Struck me so. Riled me."

"I'd hate to get you really stirred up! But the look on his face as he took off—he's in a mood to kill! And when he gets a grudge, he don't just hold it or dandle it on his knee. He feeds it on snake juice and spider bite."

Fumbling, McKay made sure of a chair and sank onto it. Reaction soured his initial sense of triumph. He had taken Connor by surprise, and once he had him in his hands, he had been in control. But that initial success would not weigh in the continuing struggle, save to increase Slash's vindictiveness.

It had been sheer chance that Jim O'Donnell happened along at so vital a moment. Otherwise, the returning crew might have only guessed at the sequence of events—the broken window, his own lifeless body. But suspicion would not have restored him to life or brought his slayer to justice.

And Slash, as O'Connell warned, cherished a grudge.

McKay had never backed away from a fight, but a contest in the open, man to man, was one thing. Treachery in the dark—and his night stretched on endlessly—there was the whisper of terror.

"Want me to put a new window in place?" O'Donnell asked. "Keep out the flies and mosquitoes. And you might need another for target practice!"

12

Slash was almost home before his anger cooled to a point where he could think objectively. Then he realized that, bruised and cut, smeared with dried blood, he must appear not only fearsome but the loser of whatever bout he had engaged in. It would be foolish to appear before Cleone in so unfavorable a light.

He halted at a creek to wash the blood from his

hands and face, wondering how to explain a mishap he could not conceal. He might, of course, say nothing, but such silence would lead to speculation, probably unfavorable.

To his surprise, Cleo asked no questions. She stared as he entered the house, then turned with prompt decisiveness to the kitchen cupboard and its small stock of salves and medicines.

"Sit here and let me clean those cuts," she instructed, and Slash obeyed, reveling in such treatment as he had never before experienced. Of course, as his sister...

Cleo filled a basin with hot water from the big teakettle, then wrung out a cloth and set about the ministering. Slash slumped back, yielding to the luxury. Lame muscles, the result of his headlong exit through the window, warned him that he would be stiff and sore for a while, but by the time the cuts healed he would be as good as ever.

"That feels nice," he mumbled. By way of explanation he said, "My horse jumped at something—piled me right into a thorn bush. It didn't make for a comfortable landing."

"I should think not." His explanation was possible if not probable. Cleo was resolved to ask no questions, make no demands, until she had a better understanding of this man who was supposedly her brother and partner in a big ranch. Somehow each part seemed less possible as time went on. What had begun as a wild fancy was changing to a bad dream, one that would have seemed impossible except that she was a part of it.

Since Slash was her brother—if he actually was—it seemed that she should feel some sense of kinship, an awakening of blood ties, at least a beginning of friendship along with acquaintance. So far there had been nothing of the kind. She gave Slash credit for a casual if detached politeness, but that should be accorded any guest. There had been nothing more. He had asked no questions, shown no curiosity about her or their mother or those lost years in which she had not even suspected his existence.

More and more she felt like a bystander, almost an interloper. The only two persons who had been friendly and helpful since she had stepped from the stage were the clerk and Dave McKay. Her thoughts were more and more of him. She wanted to ask if there was any news of him since his fearful mishap. She was reasonably certain that Slash had come from the direction of Lost Horse and, with a sudden sense of fear, wondered if his mishap might have some connection.

But already she had learned that Slash counted the owner of the Lost Horse as an enemy. Had the two of them clashed, despite McKay's blindness?

Her fingers, sure until then, faltered. Slash stirred and opened his eyes. Such womanly ministrations were as new as they were welcome, but the touch of kindness had served to make up his mind. Cleo was not his sister, and for that he was thankful. How he was to explain the true but altered status would take some figuring out.

Most of the fault, along with the background, could be placed where it rightly belonged, on Longpre Connor, who at the last had not hesitated to admit his guilt.

Once Cleo was his wife, past difficulties and the problem of ownership of the ranch would be resolved. Supremely self-satisfied with his sudden decision, forgetful of how he had been manhandled that afternoon, no shadow of doubt bothered Slash. Not only was he in control of a big spread, which he intended should soon be doubled in size, but he was Slash Connor.

To his mind, it followed as night followed day that any woman whom he deigned to ask would be more than pleased to marry him.

13

Life went on, but it was existence now rather than living. No longer was each day a fresh adventure, its challenges a joyous experience. The most frustrating part to Dave McKay was his dependence upon others. He had been self-reliant, but now he was checked and circumscribed even in thinking or planning.

I'll have to have a lawyer, he decided. And there

again was the frustration, since Phineas Chadwin was the only attorney within reach and not a man McKay would ordinarily pick or trust. But he could draw up papers, which could be read back by men McKay could trust and, once signed, they would provide legal barriers. Without those, if something happened to him—in addition to what had already hit him—victory for Slash would come too easily.

I can manage it, with witnesses, he reflected. And the sooner matters are down in black and white, the better.

He would have preferred to ride with O'Donnell, but when he shouted for O'Brion and instructed him to have horses saddled and call for Jim, Baldy replied that the cowboy was working miles away, in a direction opposite from town.

"I sent him to hunt some strays," he explained guilelessly, and again McKay knew the bitterness of his imprisonment. On the chance that he might want him, O'Brion had made sure that Jim would be out of reach.

"In that case, you'll have to ride to town with me," McKay returned. "We've things to tend to."

The foreman favored him with a sharp, suspicious stare, which McKay could not see. McKay had wanted O'Donnell, not himself, as guide, but he had acquiesed too readily. Like a fox, O'Brion was by nature suspicious, inclined always to look for a trap. So speedy a return to town, with its possible implications, worried him. The Old Man was by way of making medicine.

McKay had not been the only one to be taken by surprise, caught off guard by his sudden blindness. To O'Brion it had been equally unlooked for. Since it had happened, it presented opportunities that must not be wasted.

He was still foreman, and by doing a good job, serving loyally, he might take over the complete running of the ranch, with all its attendant chances. The temptation was strong. His trouble was that he had not foreseen such a break when selling his services to Slash Connor. He had sold them on an all-out basis and was in too deep to draw back. Slash's interests must come first.

And whatever McKay had in mind would involve Slash. It was all-out war between them, and regardless of his eyes, McKay's brain was not impaired.

While riding, O'Brion's conviction strengthened. He could not take chances nor afford any to McKay. He had been taking Slash Connor's pay for almost as long as he had worked at Lost Horse, and the time had come to earn some of that easy money.

They jogged side by side, each busy with his own thoughts. The sun fell warmly on McKay's face, yet as he stared with open eyes, he caught no glimpse of light. He had a sense of double blindness, of a wall solid, immovable.

However, the situation was not as hopeless as it had seemed. His other senses were taking over, a sharpening of instinct along with a keenness of insight. It was clear that Shaney had not been the only man on his crew who was in the pay of an enemy. His foreman could not, would not have passed up such an opportunity. A score of happenings over the past months, each small and isolated in itself, took on new and significant meaning when put together, forming as a whole a conclusive pattern that could not be doubted.

So he must deal with O'Brion. After this visit to a lawyer, it would be the next order of business. He would have to replace him, since he had to be surrounded by men he could trust to operate the ranch.

But where to find a foreman with the necessary qualifications? By training and talent, Baldy was ideally equipped for managing so big an outfit. Jim O'Donnell, his next and inevitable choice because of loyalty, was a good cowhand.

But that was all. Loyal. A good cowhand. But no executive, certainly no manager.

And now, more than ever, he needed a take-charge man.

Baldy was chattering like a magpie, flitting like an excited bird from branch to branch, subject to subject. Ahead, the trail branched, and it had suddenly occurred to him that McKay might sense any turn or swing unless his attention was distracted. Forcing his own horse from the main road with an iron hand, O'Brion reached with his other to grasp the bridle of McKay's, just short of the bit, causing the horse to follow instead of holding along the familiar road to town. Relieved that his ruse had worked, Baldy fell silent. Apparently the change in pace had been so slight that the blind man had failed to notice it.

Here Baldy was both correct and yet in error. The hesitation and turning of his horse had escaped even McKay's heightened senses, but all at once the sun was upon his face from a different angle. He puzzled over that, uncertainly trying to judge. Hereabouts the road ran straight—but now there were turns and twists, factors suddenly noticeable, full of hidden but certain meaning.

Baldy was suddenly voluble again, but he was no actor. Tension vibrated in his voice.

"Just in case you're wondering," he said, "we've left the road and are on the path to the Three X. It just struck me like it'd be a good idea, since it ain't much out of our way. With you the way you are, we can't afford trouble. Now's the time for you and Connor to talk things over, with me to sort of ride herd and keep him reined in. Get matters straightened out before they get worse."

Before McKay could reply, O'Brion raised his voice in a hail.

"Howdy, Slash. We figured to drop by—talk things over and see if we can't get them set right."

His tone was carefully casual, but Slash, surprised and as startled at this sudden visit as McKay, could not miss the elaborate wink of an eye. Since McKay could not see, it was safe enough and afforded ample explanation. O'Brion was informing him that McKay had been on his way to town, and O'Brion had decided that he must not reach it.

What action Connor might decide to take now was up to him.

Slash was sufficiently quick of wit to understand, to appreciate what Baldy was trying to do. What O'Brion could not understand was the sudden fury in Slash's face, a bitter anger directed toward himself. He had been intent to get in his explanation before McKay or Slash could balk or stop it, too eager to speak his piece to notice that Cleo Connor loitered in the background, watching with increasing surprise and not only able to hear but to see that meaningful droop of the eyelid that was concealed from McKay.

Had any doubt remained, O'Brion's careful timing confirmed McKay's suspicions, rousing his anger along with apprehension. Baldy had deliberately tricked him, leading him into the enemy's camp. Now they believed—perhaps rightly—that they had him trapped. Yesterday, for a short while, he had been able to turn the tables on Connor, but this was Slash's home ground. With the situation reversed, Slash was not likely to be in a forgiving mood.

"You're a fool, Baldy," McKay said flatly. "If I'd wanted to come here, I'd have said so."

Baldy smirked. The better he understood, the more Slash could appreciate the situation.

The gesture seemed to freeze on his face at the prompt, unequivocal agreement Slash voiced.

"Yeah, you sure are a fool, O'Brion. We talked yesterday—and if McKay wanted to come here, he'd have told you."

Taken aback, Baldy was less nimble of wit than usual. That Slash might be talking for the benefit of his sister, desperately anxious to erase any possible thought she might have of his implication, did not occur to O'Brion. That Slash, on his own land, might be influenced by anyone, much less a woman, was too wild a notion to credit. Baldy had made it as clear as he knew how that the situation had become grim if not desperate and that McKay must be dealt with.

Slash understood what Baldy was trying to tell him and its importance. Under any other circumstance he would have responded in kind. But McKay had given Cleo a ride out from town, and she had helped him when he was in desperate straits. And though she had not said much, it was clear to Slash that she sympathized with McKay in his sudden affliction, and pity was akin, if not to love, at least to liking.

Such feelings on her part were perhaps sudden, but to Slash they were understandable. To his increasing amazement, he knew that he was as suddenly if inexplicably in love with her. Even thinking of her, his emotions were so tangled that he could hardly sort them out or even wish to. She, and his feelings for her, were something apart from all else.

Above all, he had to find a way to untangle a badly twisted situation, to reasonably explain their relationship—or lack of it—so that he could make her his wife. And that, he knew, he would do for her own sake, not considering the uncontested title to the ranch she would bring as a dowry.

Not that the ranch and its title would not be welcome. But for once Slash was stirred by higher motives.

Sympathizing as Cleo did with McKay, she would resent any unfairness toward him, and might even hate Slash if she learned of the conspiracy, the treachery of a double cross, and the coldly brutal action that O'Brion was suggesting to him, not too subtly. The blundering fool—

Slash caught himself, reining in his temper with difficulty. He dared not say too much.

"Maybe we can have a talk and thresh matters out, McKay, one of these days," he added. "But not now or by any duress. I knew nothing of this, and I'm sorry that your man has tricked you, even with the best of intentions." He swung to O'Brion.

"Since you're acting as guide, do a proper job. Take him on to town or back home—whichever he prefers. And while it's hardly for me to give you orders, I suggest that you make sure that he gets where he's supposed to go."

This time, with his back turned squarely to Cleo, Slash was able to return the wink, with all its implications. O'Brion, he knew, was not so stupid as to fail to understand. Slash's words had been explicit, before witnesses. They bespoke good will on his part, along with orders that nothing should go amiss where McKay was concerned.

That they also carried a double meaning was made explicit by the wink.

O'Brion understood, even though Slash's reasons were unclear. It wasn't like Slash to be squeamish, even of an occasional murder, but Slash was the boss.

There were still long miles between this spot and town—ample time and opportunity, in wild country, for Baldy to do what he had been suggesting should be done, to earn the easy money he had been pocketing for so long.

Unwillingly he realized that the responsibility had been shoved on to him; the suspicion when McKay failed to return alive from a ride would attach to him. Too late he recognized the caliber of the man whose money he had taken. Slash was not the fool he appeared. When he paid for something, he expected to receive full value in return.

14

O'Brion was thankful for only one thing, and not much of that. Sightless as he was, McKay could not see his face or the mixture of dismay and anger that showed livid. Not that the lack of vision would make much difference. McKay's brain was unquestionably as lively as before, and he would put words and events together, understanding not only what had transpired but what was slated to happen.

His position was unenviable. But Baldy's was nothing to write home about.

O'Brion seized on the opening Slash had given him, talking fast and as convincingly as he could manage.

"I'm sorry I bungled things, coming off this way. I guess I should have asked you, but I didn't think you'd agree, and it seemed like it was worth a try. And I do think it put him in a more reasonable mood. But since you don't feel that way..."

McKay scarcely heard. There were certain compensations for his blindness—his remaining senses were becoming increasingly acute. O'Brion was in Connor's pay, as he had suspected for some time and now knew beyond any doubt. Baldy had expected to please his real boss by delivering McKay into his power. What he had overlooked was that it might prove an embarrassment of riches.

Slash's reaction, and the reason for it, was clear enough. In no case could he afford so public a disclosure of treachery and its planned aftermath, with several of his own crew probably on hand as witnesses. It was also possible that Cleo had overheard. But his insistence that O'Brion make sure of McKay's safety was overdone. He protested too much.

The ironic part of McKay's insight and understanding was that it left him as helpless as before. Aware that he would be riding into danger, he had no chance to see, no way of avoiding it. Connor's insistence had emphasized the opposite of what he had said. McKay was not to reach town or to return home.

Ostensibly, Baldy O'Brion was still working for him as protector and guide. Actually he was captor and guard. The initiative lay with him, to pick and choose the time, place, and method. McKay could not escape, either on horseback or by plunging away on foot. Blindness was an all but total fetter. Unable to tell when or where the "accident" would happen, McKay's mind roamed.

There were plenty of possibilities from which O'Brion might choose. A bullet, possible drowning in the waters of the Lost Horse, any number of accidents along the trail. The only thing McKay could be sure of was that, when it came, the stroke would be swift and deadly, hard to parry even if he was prepared.

Baldy was not apt to use a gun, for a bullet would leave the earmarks of murder. He was badly flustered by Slash's angry rejection of his plan, almost equally furious with both his employers, but not to the extent that he would lose his head and leave such evidence as a gunshot against himself. He would work to contrive an accident—and the country ahead abounded in opportunities.

Again McKay thought of his helplessness.

Eyesight was a measureless blessing, one that he had taken for granted while he possessed it, never really comprehending what it amounted to.

He could still feel the sun, warm against his face and hands, bringing a sudden popping of sweat to his horse's glossy coat. The wetness had a sticky quality under his fingertips. They were climbing, the ponies forced to greater exertion.

Added proof was the pungent aroma of evergreen—pine and spruce, which clustered in groves across the high country. To the faint jingle of bit and spur was added the rattle of shod hoofs across rocky ground, a small medley that usually went unnoticed, but now was sharp with meaning.

They had been riding again for perhaps half an hour and would be well beyond sight and sound from road or buildings. Steel-shod hoofs slipped and ground on the increasingly rocky trail. The outline of what O'Brion intended was clear enough. The actual time and place had to be remote, beyond any chance witness or easy discovery.

For a while O'Brion had talked, breathing fervent protests and disclaimers. These had trailed to silence as he received no reply, finally realizing that he was not fooling McKay. Or even himself.

The flow of words had been intended to bolster his own resolution as much as anything for the job he had to do. All at once he was mired in a grim, deadly business, in far deeper than he had ever expected or intended, compelled to a chore not only repugnant but for which he knew himself to be ill fitted.

The trouble was that he had trapped himself as surely as he had McKay. He could neither escape nor evade. He had to go through with it.

Like McKay, he could think of several almost perfect places for the staging of a murderous accident, remote among the hills, beyond all sight or sound. Places where, once a man disappeared, he was unlikely ever to be found.

Suspicion, Baldy realized, would inevitably attach to him when he returned from this ride without his employer. Suspicion that could ostracize him from the only society he knew, his explanations or excuses ringing hollow.

Or must they? O'Brion sucked in a sudden breath as a solution came to him. He could admit at least some of the truth, while enlarging upon the accident that was to happen. If he too was a part of it, and was hurt while trying to save or help McKay, and afterward led a rescue party...

A rescue that would inevitably be too late, to a dead and broken body.

If he returned home properly bruised and bloody, some might still harbor suspicions, but most men would credit him with having done his best. Accidents—a horse slipping or becoming panicky and bolting—did happen on such trails.

No one except Slash Connor would know the real background or guess the truth. And it would suit Slash to back him, since he was carrying out Slash's orders.

He would have been startled had he guessed how well McKay understood his plan, how well he knew where they were. There were no such stretches of rocky trail on the way to town or back to the Lost Horse. They were on a shortcut between the two ranches, a trail that saved miles. McKay had occasionally taken it, but it was rarely used. Not only was it dangerous but, twisting and climbing, it took more time than the wider, easier route.

Both the horses were straining, scrambling up a steep incline. They reached a crest, and the muted sound of a waterfall broke against the silence. Hearing it, McKay knew almost exactly where they were. Higher crests reared beyond, but this was the top of the trail. Any sensible man, using this route, dismounted and led his horse, not just out of consideration for the animal, but to minimize the risk of falls.

O'Brion continued to ride, risking the danger, not daring to allow McKay to dismount. He did permit the winded animals a brief pause, their heavy blowing almost the only sound. McKay's ears crackled at the elevation. O'Brion's horse pawed nervously. Otherwise the silence held.

In a fever of impatience, O'Brion spurred harder than he had intended. His horse jumped and plunged, and Baldy, knowing there was sparse room for gyrations, only heart-stopping distances below, frantically reined him in. He was too far along to alter his plan or turn back. He knew that McKay understood, sensing that he was on a ride with only one ending.

Watching him, O'Brion shivered nervously. McKay was easy yet rocklike in the saddle, betraying no apprehension, disdaining to beg or plead for a mercy he knew would not be granted. The iron nerve of the blind man made Baldy's fears worse. Somehow this whole thing was incredible. He had to finish, to get out of this before his own nerve cracked, to keep from giving way to an increasing impulse to jump or plunge, screaming, into the yawning depths to the side.

Ahead the trail straightened out, leveling, clinging to the side of the mountain, increasingly narrow. Not daring to look down, Baldy trusted to his horse. Height always made him dizzy, sometimes to the point of sickness. He almost envied McKay his blindness.

He had taken this route once before, promising himself never to do so again. But at that time he hadn't envisioned the present need, along with the many opportunities the steep, narrow trail offered.

From the depths below reflected a splash of silver—sun on Lost Horse Creek. Save for that single spot, the stream was veiled, shut off by the surrounding heights and the massive depths of the canyon, with its shroud of evergreens.

Now! Here was as good a place as any, as likely a spot as might be found. According to the terrain, O'Brion by turns had led or driven McKay's cayuse. With the narrowing or widening of the trail it pressed ahead as opportunity offered, more than eager to have for itself what inadequate space there was.

Again O'Brion drove in the spurs, a gesture he could not restrain, as savage as it was sudden. It sent his pony plunging ahead, crowding instinctively to the inner side along the wall between the cliff and the other horse—two frantic creatures, contesting where there was room only for one.

McKay rode tense, poised for action. Knowing what had become inevitable, he realized that his chance for action, his hope for survival, was as slight as it was desperate. But there was a chance, and his senses telegraphed the warning as he felt the plunge of the other animal smashing against his own pony in its wild rush.

O'Brion had the inner edge, a high sheer wall of rock lifting above. Opposite was a yawning emptiness broken by the reaching tops of spruce and fir. From above they had a feathery, almost gossamer look. More were below, toward the remote river, depths insubstantial yet somehow solid, known to the hawk and eagle.

McKay's reaching hands found a grip and clutched. At such a time and spot a man could only do his best, and probably it would not be good enough. But if he was to die he intended to take his killer with him. Here his lack of sight was at least as much an asset as hindrance. He had none of O'Brion's almost gibbering terror of the depths.

After the long climb, the slow drag of suspense, the climax was swift. McKay's wildly scrambling cayuse screamed, a high neigh of terror as its hoofs slid and it was crowded from the slippery rock where only a mountain goat would feel at home.

A matching cry bubbled from O'Brion's lips as hands clutched and dragged. With the weight both of McKay and his falling horse and the impetus of the plunge, O'Brion was torn from his saddle, pulled along with McKay.

Baldy had no time to reflect that his scheme was working almost to perfection, at least in the initial stages; even he was becoming a part of the accident in convincing fashion. He was past reason or thinking, scream upon scream torn from his throat as he sensed the clutch of the depths.

McKay, still holding grimly, falling, accepted

the result almost fatalistically. He was doing what was possible, and he had hardly hoped for better.

Somewhere, like an echo, it seemed as though another wild cry came back, but that was as unlikely as it was inconsequential.

15

More shaken than he cared to admit, Slash Connor turned away, managing an almost casual nod to Cleo. *The bungling fool,* he reflected furiously, but on the whole he felt that he had carried matters off very well. The situation had arisen suddenly, fraught with possibilities for disaster or at least for a high degree of unpleasantness.

"That foreman of McKay's means well, I suppose, but he gets some funny notions," he observed. "I expect what he really had in mind was to have us talk and make McKay listen to reason whether he liked it or not. To more or less compel a solution." His headshake was almost admiring.

"Maybe he had a point. But I guess he forgot that we'd continue to be neighbors and have to keep on living in the same country. Well, life goes on, and there's work to be done."

Cleone was spared the need for a reply as Slash and his men rode away, taking an almost opposite direction from that chosen by O'Brion. Their almost uneasy haste left her to her own devices. She had been planning on a ride, though with no particular destination in mind. Now, automatically, she made up her mind.

Within moments, thankful for her riding skill, she was bridling and saddling a horse. She mounted rapidly.

Slash had been right—his back was to her when he had returned O'Brion's wink with a broadly expressive gesture of his own. What Connor had failed to note was Baldy's answering wink, intended to convey his understanding—missed by Slash, but caught by Cleo.

Still far from understanding all that was going on, she knew a lot and sensed more. Something as sinister as it was dark was being played out on this range of the Lost Horse, a plot somehow directed against Dave McKay in which Slash Connor was involved.

By rights, she supposed that her sympathies as well as her own concerns and fortunes should lie with Slash and the Triple X—this ranch so sardonically known across the whole range as Triple Cross.

But her initial doubt of this newly discovered brother had increased to distrust. At the same time, her sympathies were engaged by McKay and the fight he was making against odds as unusual as they were incredible; a contest, she knew now, for survival, for life itself.

Words had been spoken, pious protestations intended to fool her but certainly not others. McKay had asked his foreman to guide him into town, an order that had been disobeyed in a manner so sly and secretive as to be highly revealing. O'Brion had brought McKay to Slash, not to talk matters over but as a sacrificial offering, a prisoner to be disposed of.

She had a desperate, appalled conviction that he would have been accepted and dealt with had not O'Brion blundered in overlooking her or in his assumption that her loyalty to Slash and the Triple Cross could be taken for granted.

The rest of the interchange was just as understandable. Her brother—somehow it seemed impossible that they could be related—had ordered O'Brion to take McKay away and dispose of him. The actual meaning seemed only too plain.

She had no plan, no notion of what she might attempt to do to thwart such a plot or help McKay, but once in the saddle, she followed as fast and as well as she could. It was not easy. She had been delayed by saddling a horse and the increasing brush and trees on the hills that quickly led into mountains slowed and hindered her.

Twice she feared that she had lost them, then distant glimpses enabled her to hold the trail and gradually to gain. The nature of the terrain, the brutal heights and dizzy depths at either side, warned her of what impended. O'Brion was not guiding McKay to town or ranch but to his death. An accident, in such country...

Her hope was that she might come close enough to make her presence known so that Baldy would abandon whatever he planned. She refused to think that she might be risking a matching peril by cornering a killer, just as she centered her attention on what was ahead rather than on the frightening aspects of the trail. She had to help McKay.

Sudden wild screams, from horse and man, along with a glimpse of the struggle and the figures spilling from the trail, brought an answering cry of dismay from her own throat. She was too late.

Blindness was a fetter, but it carried certain compensations. O'Brion's gusty breathing and jittery responses warned McKay that these heights and depths had reduced him to a state of near collapse. McKay was spared that ordeal, though he had never been much bothered by heights.

But his knowledge of what was below, beneath the trail, was chilling enough. Somewhere hereabouts would be the chosen spot, the climactic moment. But he was given no time for thinking.

The suddenly crowding cayuse, his own desperate clutch, and then he was falling. Branches enveloped him, the close-growing tops of a spruce checking his plunge, then bouncing him to one side. Almost at once he felt the ground again as he sprawled on a rocky surface, gasping for breath. Sounds continued, welling up from below—the crashing of heavy bodies falling unchecked amid and through barriers of branches, and then sudden silence.

Even without such an indicator he knew that he was alone, that O'Brion had torn loose from his grasp at the first impact. On one point Baldy's judgment had been excellent. It was a likely spot for a fatal accident.

Silence—the quiet of the high country, where only the winds moved. He caught the sigh of the distant waterfall, contrasting with the suck and murmur of Lost Horse Creek far below. Shock ebbed, the sudden pain to bruised flesh subsided, and he considered this piece of incredible luck— though whether it was astonishingly good or horribly bad was a matter for speculation.

He was alive and unhurt instead of broken flesh far below. For the moment that rated as a plus. The thick tops of a tree had caught and checked him, then bounced him away. Again, when he might have continued the plunge, he had landed on some sort of shelf, a jarring fall but too short to do more than shake him.

His questing fingers encountered empty space, which was what he had expected. Such a jut or outcrop would not extend far. He could envision the sheer cliff above, probably unclimbable to the trail even if he could see. Descent to the creek under such conditions was equally out of the question.

Even without memory, the ascending sounds warned of the depths from which they came. The birds that swam the air currents of the canyon— hawk and eagle, kingfisher and crow—would soar high, but well below him.

The chance of being found and helped he dismissed as out of the question. No one, with the exception of Slash Connor, would have expected them to come this way. Even if a search was conducted among these hills, the odds against finding him were ten thousand to one. Even a rider, passing at the point where he had gone off the trail, would be unlikely to spot him on a half-hidden shelf somewhere below.

This was like a mocking replay of that other day when he had been swept from his horse by the low limb of a tree, left lost and alone. But that time he had had a fighting chance on solid, open ground, rather than trapped with nowhere to go.

And that time Cleo had found him.

He couldn't hope for such luck again, from her or anyone. And as he wet his suddenly dry lips and sought to accept that certainty, Cleo called, her voice quavering between hope and despair.

"Dave! Oh God, help him—help me! David McKay!"

He jerked involuntarily, tensing as a hand and arm slid and encountered emptiness. Cautiously he drew back. He had not dreamed it—that was her voice from somewhere along the trail above. He realized that she had followed them and must be at or near the point where he, O'Brion, and the horse had gone off. Whether she had seen that fall or was merely noticing the scarred sign he didn't know. She sensed what had happened and was despairing with realization.

Hope was a sudden tonic. McKay returned the hail.

"Cleo! Be careful! I'm down here—on a shelf of rock or something."

Her startled exclamation was between astonishment and relief. She had cried out in despair rather than from any hope; nothing could take such a plunge and live.

As McKay cautioned her against a slip, she dismounted and tried to see, to peer straight down to half-screened depths that still were open enough to make the senses reel. To her gasping relief she glimpsed a leg and, though not fully understanding, lost no time in planning his rescue.

"Are you hurt, David? Bleeding or broken?"

"Nothing worse than a few bruises," he assured her. "I'll be all right—I'll sit here and wait while you go for help."

She doubted that. Here blindness was an asset—a look down might have brought overwhelming dizziness and a slip and plunge. But the outcrop or shelf on which he had fallen was small enough, and he might be more badly hurt than he admitted.

"In that case, I think I can reach you with the lariat on my saddle. Tie it about your waist when I lower it."

He was too relieved to argue. "No trouble there. Only make sure you don't slip. Use your horse and saddle to hoist me."

"I will." Her voice was controlled, soft with relief. How it could have happened, when she had despaired of any chance, was not important. What counted was that he was alive, though in so precarious a position that he must be rescued as soon as possible.

McKay forced himself to relax, distributing his bulk more evenly on the stone. From above came small noises as Cleo made her preparations, then a sudden despairing wail.

"It's not long enough—"

Then almost immediately she called again.

"But it doesn't matter. The other horse can't have gone far. I'll get the rope from that saddle—your saddle? The two will reach. And I'll hurry."

She was confused about which horse had been forced off the trail, but O'Brion's, riderless, had probably stopped as soon as it reached a wider spot. Most horses would stand hitched when the reins were dropped.

A kingfisher squawked in sudden fury, and McKay guessed that it had made its plunge into deep waters, emerging with a captive fish, only to have a watchful hawk pounce in freebooting attack. The wild was fair but coldly impartial.

Cleo was back within minutes, assuring him that she had the extra rope. Moments later the end of the lariat slapped across his ankle, and he reached cautiously and grasped it. Looping the rope under his arms, he tied it, and then she was back in her saddle, moving the horse carefully, gradually hoisting him with the climb of the trail.

Struggling to keep himself away from the rocky wall, he finally felt solid ground beneath his feet. Then, with a cry, Cleo was beside him, her arms clasping him possessively.

16

They rode most of the way back in silence,
McKay mounted on O'Brion's horse. Working
down from the high country, Cleo again was guide
and mentor.

Assured that he had not been seriously injured,
she left him at his door, glancing dubiously at the
huge sprawl of the house, a half sob in her throat at
the thought of him alone in the darkened building.

The unbroken silence indicated that the crew had not yet returned.

"Will you be all right?" she asked. "I—I'd better get back before I'm missed."

"I'll be fine, thanks to you." He added huskily, "You've been my guardian angel, Cleo—and angel is the right word."

"We've both been lucky—finding each other." Her laugh was shaky. "So much of this has been so awful. I hope there won't be any more difficulty— or trouble..." Her whisper trailed to silence, remembering the talk earlier in the day, words so promising yet false.

"I'd like to settle any differences by talking them out," McKay returned soberly, but the same memory was like a mockery. "If Slash was only like you! Somehow you don't fit in the picture with such a family. Not any part of it."

"Perhaps because I was raised apart, and differently," she returned. "Please be careful. Doubly careful."

There would be speculation about what had happened to Baldy, but even Slash would hardly guess the truth. The knowledge that joined McKay and Cleo would be unsafe for additional sharing.

He heard her ride away and then went inside, into the familiar house that was no longer a haven, only a shelter. She should not be returning to Triple Cross, but there was nothing that he could do or say. Again the impulse to strike out savagely had to be conquered. The frustration of helplessness was the worst.

Toby returned and set about preparations for supper, cheerfully unaware that anything unusual had happened. Then, as a knock sounded and O'Donnell hailed and let himself in, McKay sensed a hidden meaning in his casual question.

"You all right, Dave?"

"A bit short as to sight, Jim. Otherwise I couldn't be better. Something on your mind?"

"Quite a bit." His ears told him that O'Donnell had helped himself to a chair. "Some ways, you've had a hard run of luck. But others, like today—it strikes me that the lady's gone a long way to make up for some of the bad."

"I'll go along with that. What's on your mind?"

"Just that I saw quite a bit of what happened today. I was too far away to take a hand, riding to clean out a spring, but I heard the yells when your horse and Baldy went off the cliff. Didn't see it happen, but I got a good notion of what and where. Then the little lady came along, and I saw how she rescued you. I'd sure have tried to lend a hand, since I was within half a mile, only it took a good three miles of climbing and circling to reach the place, as I found out."

He took a long moment for thought. "I'd begun

to figure Baldy for a skunk, though I hadn't had a notion of just how bad."

"Once an egg spoils, it can end up mighty rotten."

"Yeah, it makes a skunk smell almost sweet by comparison. You folks were gone by then, so I worked back up the creek along the canyon. Not so mean a route as the high one, but wet and nasty. Couldn't find the horse, but I did come upon Baldy. He was layin' half in and half out of the water. Head and shoulders under."

"Poor devil."

"Easy and quick—some better than a rope, I guess. Not far off, there was an overhang to the bank. I used my shovel to spill it over him. Better than what he deserved."

"You did the decent thing."

"Might save questions, sometime. Not that they'd matter too much. Makes three of us as witnesses to what happened if it was ever needed. You and me and the little lady. Though I don't reckon it'll ever come to that."

Nor did McKay. People would speculate and wonder, but not much. Slash Connor's curiosity would be the liveliest, but he had covered his own trail as carefully as a fox at the scene of its latest raid when Baldy O'Brion had last been seen in public. Knowing what Baldy had had in mind, he would not be inclined to question or to delve very deeply.

Even had he felt strongly about the matter or been inclined to betray curiosity, Slash found his attention diverted, not too pleasantly, that same evening. He had no inkling that trouble was coming down the trail. A horseman emerged, pulling up in the settling night, then dismounted and slouched across to knock at the door. Slash threw it open, then frowned at the man in the light of the coal-oil lamp, momentarily at a loss. Finally he recognized his caller as someone from the town, a man who clerked at the Mercantile and assisted at the post office that occupied one corner of the building.

Eyes both too small and too close together studied the cattleman slyly. Not waiting for an invitation, he entered and helped himself to a chair. He fumbled with an inside coat pocket, but then, changing his mind, withdrew the hand, empty.

"Brought you something, sort of," he explained. "Or at least, I guess it's for your sister."

Slash extended a hand. "In that case, I'll see that she gets it."

"Would you, now? Or maybe you'd as soon she didn't have such a letter to read. Might give her notions."

"What the devil are you driving at?" Connor's temper was fraying as night drew on. Even Cleo was absent, and while that could hardly have any connection with the ride taken by Baldy O'Brion and his prisoner, the day had been nerve-racking enough without having to worry about her whereabouts. "If you have a letter—"

"Oh; I have the letter right enough. Maybe you don't remember, but I work at the store—help now and then with the mail. Name of Sanders. G. Sanders."

"I remember. They call you Grubby."

The little eyes took on a reddish gleam. Sanders was accustomed to being kicked around, but even a cur could snarl and bite.

"Like I say, I've got a letter—addressed to Miss Cleone Connor, from a point back east. I remember about it because your pa dropped it in the box not too long before he kicked the bucket. Bought the stamp to send it from me. So I sort of noticed as he dropped it through the slot, it being the only one. I picked it up and put it with the other outgoing mail. So when it came back, after a spell, marked 'Return to Sender,' why I noticed that it was the same one."

Slash listened impatiently, but with a growing sense of trouble. "All right," he growled. "Since it's hers, give it here."

"No hurry. The fact of the matter is, I didn't

bring it with me. Got to thinking, and left it in a safe place—just in case. From the look of it, it must have had kind of a rough trip there and back. The envelope was torn, quite a big rip. And the paper inside was halfway sticking out—"

"So you read it! Didn't your boss ever tell you what the penalty is for interfering with the mail?"

"My job's to look after the mail, ain't it? And who's to know? I'm not blabbing to anybody else, and I don't figure you will."

Slash restrained his temper. Clearly the letter had been written by Longpre Connor, but dispatched too late, as events had outrun it. Judging by the repentant mood that had come upon Longpre near the end, as he sensed his early demise, having broken a lifetime of silence, there was no telling what he might have said.

"All right, it's your story," Slash spit out through gritted teeth. "You're telling it."

"Yeah, I sure am. And in that letter, your old dad told some things, too. About how he'd stole another man's wagon and ranch and even his name, back when you and this Miss Cleo was just toddlers, and how he felt bad about that and wanted to try and right those wrongs, as much as he could. That letter makes it clear that the Triple Cross belongs to Miss Cleo—even if she don't know it—and not to you at all."

Slash was appalled though not much surprised.

The old fool had really messed things up with that final gesture. Slash had no doubt that Grubby was telling the truth, since it coincided with what he knew. Such a letter, in the wrong hands, could mean ruin.

He should be able to counter any effect on Cleone by marrying her, as he had already decided to do. But the danger, with a rat like Sanders, was that he might show it to others.

Grubby's cunning might fall well short of a fox's, but he was in a strong bargaining position and knew it. Should anything happen to him, the letter would probably turn up, along with a message implying Slash's responsibility for whatever "accident" might have happened.

Just when he had disposed of McKay and the way seemed clear, he was neck-deep in trouble.

"All right, we understand each other," he granted. "I might dicker for that letter and the trouble you've been put to. Let's be generous and say a h—"

Reading the mocking glitter in those small eyes, he gulped and revised his offer upward. "Say a thousand dollars."

Grubby's derisive cackle assured him that he had blundered, placing his foot squarely in the trap. Now it was blackmail, and Sanders understood the potential fully. Here at long last was not only a chance for big money, but an opportunity to get back at some of the representatives of the society he hated—people who treated him with condescending scorn, or worse, ignored him as beneath contempt. And Slash Connor, boss of Triple Cross, was a perfect representative with which to deal, to force him to eat dirt in turn.

"A thousand dollars—to let you hang on to a place worth fifty times as much! Do you take me for a fool?"

Slash checked a too-ready admission. This man could be dangerous.

"A thousand dollars sounds like pretty good pay to me—especially when a word from me to the proper authorities could send you to the pen for tampering with the mails. But there's no point to quarreling. I'm willing to overlook a few things. And you have to deal with me because I'm the only customer you've got who'll pay you a red cent."

"I'm not so sure of that, and neither are you. I can think of several who might pay big. So it's worth a lot to you to keep this quiet. Not just chicken feed."

Slash's big hands, gripping the arm of his chair, showed white.

"I'm short-tempered," he warned. "And most people know better than to fool with me. I'll go to five thousand, but that's the limit."

To his surprise, the grubby little man was tenacious, unyielding. The haggling went on,

Slash with the despairing realization that in taking each step he irrevocably committed himself. Sanders pointed out that with all the vast potential of the land, the big ranch was worth not merely ten times five, but twice that, and he demanded forty thousand for his part.

How perilously close he came to a sudden bullet Sanders never knew. Letter or no letter, crowded like a rat into a corner, Slash was of a mood to chance it. But his memory of Baldy O'Brion and his ride with McKay restrained him. Too many straws piling all at once could be dangerous—and there were other ways.

Exercising unusual restraint, Slash inched up his own offer as Sanders made a slow drop.

He had been sure that ten thousand—the amount he had offered Dave McKay for the Lost Horse—would clinch a settlement. It was as pitifully small an amount by comparison then as now. But finally he was forced to a realization that the little man could be crowded only so far. He was certain now that Slash had no choice.

"Twenty thousand," Connor grunted, on a note of finality. He stood up, towering menacingly. "Or would you rather be booted out of this house all the way to the county line and clear out of the country?"

Such a sum was beyond his easy or immediate securing, but for all his bluster, Slash dared not risk the alternative. The offer would buy time, perhaps opportunity. Grubby accepted grudgingly.

"It'll take me a little time to raise that much," Slash pointed out. "Such cash doesn't grow on trees."

"But hang-ropes do." Sanders checked the taunt at the reddened glare in the cattleman's eyes. After all, he had done better than he had dared hope. But he could not restrain a bit of crowing.

"You'd best be about gathering it, then." He shrugged. "You get the letter when I get the cash. But if anything should happen to me in the meantime—most any sort of an accident—then it could sure enough turn up in the wrong place. And I doubt that there'd be as many mourners for your funeral, same as for your dad!"

17

It wasn't hospitality that caused Slash to step outside as he followed Sanders out of the house. He wanted to be rid of him as soon as possible. Standing in the dark beyond his door, he watched his unwelcome visitor ride away. Again his hand dropped toward his holstered gun, only to check reluctantly. The analogy to a fox was too close. He could kill Sanders, but that might well set a noose about his own neck.

He tensed at the noise of an approaching horse, wondering if Sanders was returning, then expelled his breath in a slow sigh as he recognized the slender form of Cleo, graceful even in the gloom. What was she doing riding at this hour? Fresh unease breathed in the night air.

"Where've you been, Cleo? You shouldn't be out at night. This isn't like old settled country. It's risky to ride by yourself."

"I suppose I rode a little far." Cleone had hoped to avoid an encounter. After the events on the trail, she was in no mood to explain or talk. "I'm tired. Good night."

Slash's swift reaction was anger, but he closed his mouth, questions unasked. Better to betray no anxiety or eagerness as to what might have happened, though he had expected O'Brion to report back long before. This was not the time for him to make a full confession to Cleone about himself and their relationship.

He lay awake long, gnawing his problem like a puppy worrying an overlarge bone, seeking a solution and finding none. Morning found him gray-faced. Still there was no sign of Baldy O'Brion, not even an indirect report.

As if in keeping with his change in mood, the weather had greatly changed in the past twenty-four hours. The bright sun of the past several days was gone, obscured by a thickening haze. A quickening wind moaned from the northeast, and an unseasonal chill was in the air.

Red, a burly cowboy, led a side-dancing pony from the doors of the barn, draped knotted bridle-reins over a post, and planted a big boot viciously against the expanded belly of the cayuse.

"Takes a kick every cussed morning to get him down to size," the cowboy grunted. "Sucks himself full of air as a puff adder, then lets it out after I've tightened the cinch." He gave the heavy strap of the girth a vicious jerk, then buckled it in place. "Looks like we're in for a spell of weather. The line storm, I reckon. Right about time for it."

Slash grunted, his thoughts elsewhere. Unquestionably a storm was on the way, and it could be the equinoxial change, when the sun crossed the equator, the "line." Such shifts came both spring and fall, and occasionally the weather could be severe, storms striking with an intensity usual at a much later date and lasting sometimes for days.

"Keep an eye on the cattle," he said shortly.

"Sure," Red agreed. He removed the reins from the post and swung into the saddle. "Been doing that a couple of hours already. Caught a glimpse of our blind boy out early too, off on his spread. Must have smelled the weather. Don't suppose the time of day makes much difference to him any more—or night, for that matter."

He growled with sudden savagery and was gone.

Slash stared after him, caught between disbelief and consternation. McKay! It couldn't be. And yet Red, with eyesight to rival a hawk's, was not likely to be mistaken.

Dave McKay, early abroad, instead of lying smashed and broken at the bottom of a measureless cliff! And Baldy O'Brion had not reported back. This, too, was impossible, but life was suddenly becoming a nightmare.

Ordinarily, Slash enjoyed his meals. Food had always been one of his greatest pleasures. A stack of flapjacks swimming in syrup, with a side dish of steak, would stick to a man's ribs, even if the work precluded anything more before day's end. He ate mechanically now, not even tasting. Stepping outside again, he checked at a spit of snow against his face. Spit was the word. By rights this fast-moving storm should have been rain or, at worst, heavy, wet flakes. Instead, as though in earnest of what was to come, the pellets were flinty, driving, stinging. The wind, steadily rising, writhed through the green, unfrosted leaves on trees and shrubs in a ringing crescendo of warning.

Slash glared about, appalled. He had a notion that the fearsome reputation that went with line storms sprang from perhaps one really bad one in a score of years—a blizzard straight out of the north, unexpected, devastating in effect. Such a storm would be remembered, the tales of it embellished.

And here, totally unexpected because of the mildness of the weather preceding it, was such a storm.

Red was probably right, and since this was the line storm, it was more likely to be a long one rather than a short one. Striking early and hard, it could cause more destruction and death than all the normal storms of winter.

Already the ground was white, the air choked with the flintlike pellets. Wind, raving down from the north, behaved with true blizzard savagery, whirling and gusting. The temperature was steadily dropping. It had been somewhere in the sixties when he had gone to bed. Its sting now warned of the freezing mark. By this time tomorrow it might hover at zero.

Zero, at mid-winter, would seem almost pleasant. In early fall, coming without warning or preparation, it could be worse than an added forty degrees. The howling gale doubled its calamity.

Slash started to turn back to get the rest of the crew on the move, keeping as good a watch as was possible on the stock. Then he stopped, eyes slitted against the storm, feeling a sense of inspiration that amounted almost to shock. Here, blizzard-born, was the ready-made answer. He needed only to seize the chance.

Whatever had happened on that ride into the hills, Lost Horse was lacking its foreman, and its boss, if he still lived, was blind and helpless. The storm spelled opportunity. In such a maelstrom of wind and snow, men and animals, even at close range, were dim-seen wraiths. And the cattle, stunned by such violence, would drift with the storm.

Such instinctive, plodding movement could be helped along, to some degree directed. What was there to hinder, or who? His men, sullen under such circumstances, would do his bidding, accepting it as part of the job. They could move the bulk of McKay's herd off and beyond his range under cover of the storm, and probably with no one the wiser. All trails would be covered.

Instead of allowing them to drift aimlessly, the cattle could be headed as desired, then disposed of. And in the doing, he would not only ruin McKay, but the herd should bring enough to pay the blackmail money demanded by Sanders, leaving other sources intact.

To most living creatures, this untimely blizzard might be disaster. To Slash, the line storm spelled opportunity.

This was a night for ghosts, mad spirits holding high revel, or so it sounded as the huge old house creaked and groaned to the stresses of storm. Windows rattled. A tree branch, normally clear, bent and scraped at an edge of the roof. Hard pellets battered the windows. All through the house, whisperings were magnified to sharpness, a medley mocking the greater strife that raged beyond the walls.

Lying sleepless, McKay's thoughts turned inward, as they had done increasingly of late. Ordinarily he had never been much for introspection, preferring to deal with problems as they arose, taking whatever action might be required. But that, in large part, was no longer possible.

To him the difference between night and day had been lost, though he had a notion that this was night. His other senses were increasingly acute, his mind sharp. The headaches and other discomforts had all but disappeared, proof enough to him that they had been caused by the distillation of loco administered in his coffee, perhaps over a longer period than he had guessed.

So outlandish a scheme had probably been the product of many minds—'Lias Shaney as well as Slash, along with Baldy O'Brion. No one could do more than guess at the results, which were in some aspects more appalling than outright murder. But he had to give credit for ingenuity—the attack was so devious that it was little suspected and certainly unproven.

Loco drove animals crazy. Eventually, if they continued to eat the weed, it killed them. Shaney, who had possessed just enough background in drugs to distill such a brew, and his employer had probably derived a twisted sort of pleasure from observing how he was affected. It was akin to the cold-blooded calculation of the wolf pack, hamstringing a cornered moose, then feasting on the living, helpless victim.

He had partly checkmated them, as much through luck as anything else, but Slash considered him already hamstrung, and his motives were clear. Initially he had wanted Lost Horse. Now he sought revenge for being so ingloriously manhandled, and by a blind man.

An added complication, one no one had expected, was Cleo Connor. What was her relation to Slash? They didn't look like kin. Would Slash readily give up even part-ownership of Triple Cross? He had demonstrated that he would stop at nothing to hold fast to it.

And how McKay felt for Cleo... If he was a whole man, he thought miserably, he could ride over and ask her to marry him. But to ask her to tie herself to a blind man, doomed to follow a dark trail—that was out of the question.

Who could foresee what Slash, increasingly desperate, might do? Like the wolf, he was aptly named.

O'Donnell's loud rap on the door was too unmistakable to attribute to the storm, even without his hurried, harried explanation.

"Hate to bother you, Dave, but I figured you'd

want to know. The herd's moving—drifting with the storm, same as if this was a winter blizzard. It's getting dark, and we've lost them, even short of full dark."

What he left unspoken was equally vivid. Such an unseasonable storm was likely to continue unabated for at least another day, while the cattle scattered and perished. Even if some survived, widely dispersed, the odds against their recovery would be as close to zero as the plummeting thermometer.

18

McKay tossed back the blankets, swinging long legs over the edge of the bed. He was reaching for his clothes, carefully folded over the back of a chair, before O'Donnell finished his recital. McKay had refined and ordered certain habits in his mind to enable him to move more swiftly, surer. When every piece of furniture in the house was in its place, every article of clothing or property ready to hand, he could move almost automatically.

"What do you have in mind?" O'Donnell asked, eyeing the preparations uncertainly.

"Find them," McKay said. "Fresh horses for everybody, and pack lunches in a canvas-wrapped blanket behind each saddle. We're likely to need both. Don't rush, but don't waste time."

"But—" O'Donnell blinked, appalled at the thought of his employer venturing out in such a night with the rest of them. "It ain't fit weather for you to be out...."

"I wouldn't ask the rest of you to do it while I sat by the fire. And I expect I'll be as good as any of you under these conditions."

That was probably so, for in the raging dark of such a night, they would be as blind as he. And McKay, as ever, was the boss. Minutes later, as he led the way to where the saddled horses waited, O'Donnell had a final question, half protest.

"You any notion how we can find the cattle, even if we catch up with them?"

McKay's rejoinder startled and surprised him, meager though it was as an answer.

"I have that. Neither should be too difficult."

What was happening was clear enough to him, sparked by O'Donnell's report. Though that they should miss the obvious was understandable. The trouble was that when men could use their eyes they saw only the obvious and were apt to miss the implications.

Slash Connor, dismayed as well as enraged by recent setbacks, would not be blind to the possibilities of the storm. And that explained what otherwise was incomprehensible. As sudden and vicious as the blizzard was, bitter with driving wind and sleet, it would hardly have disturbed McKay's big herd. With an eye toward the fall roundup, he had kept them fairly well bunched for the past couple of weeks, a lazily comfortable existence on excellent pasture with the waters of Lost Horse close at hand. More to the point, it was a section well protected against winter storms.

Caught in the open or along the high country, every animal would turn its back to the drive of blizzard and drift with it. But with ample shelter at hand they would more or less close ranks, huddling for mutual protection. A swift and concerted move of the whole herd, such as O'Donnell reported, could be ruled out—unless they were being persuaded, driven, guided, kept on the move by forces more relentless than even the storm.

McKay led the way, giving precise instructions for the others to keep closely bunched at his heels. To stray in the blackness of such a night could easily be fatal. Though man and horse could endure the storm, disaster might come from

anywhere—blundering over an unseen embank-
ment or plunging into icy waters; bogging down in
a deep drift or a horse slipping and falling on ice or
in mud. The list of possibilities for trouble was
long.

Wind drove with an angry whine, the sleet
stung. McKay had no trouble in understanding
how, after making sure that the herd was gone,
they had failed to find creatures that had become
almost wraithlike, blanketed like every object,
living or inanimate, in white. And they had
searched in daylight. In this total darkness they
would be helpless but for him.

Even a few weeks before such a job would have
taxed his ability, despite the fact that he had
always had an inborn sense of direction, the
instinct of the wild that migrating birds and
animals trusted without question. To storm and
chill he was well toughened. Now his senses were
better attuned than before.

Howl and twist as it did, there was a pattern to
the wind, to the bite of the sleet. Without the
distraction of trying or feeling the desperate need
to see, it was not too difficult to head as he had
determined, making the storm his guide. It was
clear that the cattle would follow the drift of the
storm. Such a course would lead away from the
towering heights where earlier in the day Baldy
O'Brion had led him.

They had already moved to comparatively open country—summer range, where except for the fact that McKay had prepared for an easier roundup, the cattle might have been widely scattered. Easy living through long hot days under the moon of summer. But a land frigid under winter winds, savage under so unseasonable an assault. Open range, where the wind blew ever more direct, pushing, shoving.

It was big country, in which a man might pass another or skirt an entire herd like ships in the night. But such chances had to be taken. Probably there was a trail of sorts right under their feet, under the scuffed and trampled snow stirred by countless hoofs. Whether or not their horses could detect it, under the ever deepening covering and the constant stirring of the wind, there was no way of telling. If they did, they gave no sign.

But the riders could proceed at a steady pace. Warmly clad, the route was chilly and uncomfortable but not impossible. The men followed McKay with an increasing if irrational conviction that the boss knew where he was going and how to get there.

Slash Connor was more bothered: He battled the darkness, striving to see where eyes were useless, hindered by the storm rather than going along with it. But those were minor problems compared to the need to keep a tired and plodding herd bunched and moving. The latter was at least half automatic, for the wind was relentless, and the sleet stung. Every animal was plastered with a matching coat, snow turned to ice and locked in long hairs, crackling with motion but relentlessly clinging.

Always, cattle were chancy critters, some as eager, as adventure-loving as some of their two-legged counterparts; others were lazy, eager to slip away or stand unnoticed to be left behind, taking a perverse delight in fooling their self-appointed, unwelcome guardians. The angry shove of the storm helped to keep them going, but only to a degree. Men and horses, guided partly by training but more by instinct, and aided by the complaining bawling from discouraged cows, were hard put to keep the herd controlled.

Ordinarily, by night and in such weather, it was a chore that Slash would have avoided. Cowhands were paid to do the hard, dirty work, and what was the good of being a boss unless you could sleep untroubled in your own bed while others struggled and froze? But this was a special occasion, one to be grasped, exploited to the utmost. One where, whatever the discomfort, he had to be on the job, even more than the rest of them.

He had to be there to receive the payoff. Under such conditions, a drifting herd of rustled cattle became a tricky commodity.

Once the idea had come to him, he had sent word as speedily as possible to another man who always had an eye open for such opportunity, who was as careless of ethics as Slash himself when profits promised to be big. There was always the possibility that his messenger might not have made it, or of some other slip, but those odds were not big enough to be worrisome. Slash fully expected to be met at the place he had designated, sometime after daylight. It was a spot well beyond either his own or Lost Horse range, but the rendezvous should still be under cover of the storm.

There, while his own tired men headed back for home and a well-earned rest, invisible as their constantly covered trail, other equally invisible riders would take charge of a strayed herd and make sure that it moved to a new destination.

By the time the storm cleared and riders ventured forth to check the welfare of the herd, only a vast snow-covered plain would remain. Trackless and empty, it would disclose nothing.

But hard cash, the price cheap for such a herd but enough for Slash's immediate needs, would have passed from the pockets of the trader to Slash. The money was the reason he had to be there, enduring the discomfort. Slash could not for

an instant envision trusting such a sum to any of
the men in his pay.

The darkness of this night was total. Only the
whiteness of the unending snow sheet, the drive of
flakes that choked the air, gave a faint illusory
light that in turn seemed to mock. It was both bane
and blessing, the problems of snow and cold and
night, of hunger and bone-crushing fatigue. The
grass underfoot, green at the last dawn, was as lost
as yesterday.

Such storms made history, landmarks in years
ordinary enough in other aspects. Bad as it was
while it lasted, the aftermath would be appalling.
Trees not yet touched by frost, brave in their
summer green, were bending and breaking under
the clinging weight of snow. Crops on farms
ravaged by the storm would suffer untimely
harvest, would be crushed and ground down. Such
grains as remained would be soaked and spoiled.

Most creatures, whether four-footed or winged,
huddled in what shelter they could find, waiting
out the storm. Predators and victims alike knew
better than to venture into such a wilderness. That
foolishness was left to man. Even the cattle would
long since have stopped their useless drift to stand
immobilized, most likely to chill and die, if
allowed to do so.

Slash was assailed by a pang almost of pity. The
dragging night was like the endless darkness in

which Dave McKay was condemned to struggle.

Finally, almost unbelievably, there was a lightening, a grayness in the east. It came tardily, so illusory that it seemed to be of two minds, whether or not to make the effort. As far as the storm was concerned, there was no slackening. Though less flinty, the snow had grown more solid, heavy. Wind continued its endless twist and shove. The mass that cushioned grass and ground hampered at every step. Drifts reared in unexpected places, traps for the unwary.

Then, for a time, as though mocking them, showing what it might do, the storm slackened and vision increased. Slash roused from a huddled apathy that matched the cows', shaking himself. Removing a mitten, he clawed at the ice that rimmed his hat and tied-down scarf, clearing a space for seeing and breathing.

Eyes widening, he stared. Then, despite the cramp of long hours and cold, he came near to jumping and shouting. Off to the side, as he had hoped but no longer really expected, exactly on time, other riders were approaching.

It was almost too perfect, but he wanted no witnesses to the final transaction should questions be asked. He dismissed his own crew in an almost guilty haste and saw them turn back, to be quickly lost in the renewed thickening of the storm.

It was only then, as the newcomers showed more plainly, that he shivered with a sudden fresh chill, recognizing the man who guided them. It was Dave McKay, with his crew from the Lost Horse.

19

No trick is more ancient than that of the mind trying to deceive itself when confronted with bad news. The refusal to face facts has prolonged hopeless wars, turned minor problems into total disasters. That trouble, unseen and unacknowledged, is nonexistent makes for a pleasant illusion, however brief.

Slash strove for such reassurance, shutting his

eyes, hoping that what he had glimpsed was due to the distorting effect of the storm, since it was so obviously impossible. But a second look was no better. That was McKay's crew, closer now, with McKay leading.

Obviously they were the wrong bunch, and he had already sent back his own crew. Even if the cattle buyer and his men should arrive belatedly, it could make no difference. Slash knew his man. Uneasily skirting the fringe of outlawry, Slash would take a reasonable risk for the prospect of a handsome profit; but from such a situation as this, with the necessity for an open fight, he would shy as violently as a cayuse from a rattlesnake coiled in its path.

McKay was blind, and therefore helpless. Despite physical proof to the contrary, Slash had clung stubbornly to that credo. That McKay should be here, leading his crew, was so far-fetched as to be impossible. Even chance couldn't have directed them.

Then came the chill realization that somehow, once again, McKay had out-thought and out-smarted him. Once more he had lost his chance.

Emotions battled for supremacy, Slash's flaring rage demanding a swift, sure settlement. Against that was the fear of consequences. He could jerk his gun and probably kill McKay before the blind man even suspected his presence or was aware of danger. And it might not be too hard to lose himself in the storm.

But a temporary reprieve would be the best that he could hope for. If he escaped the hail of bullets McKay's outraged crew would send at him, he would still be finished on this range, outlawed, hunted. He would lose not only his ranch and the Lost Horse he was gambling for, but hc would lose Cleo.

Kicking his horse into motion, he was thankful for the renewed sweep of storm. A mile farther along he overtook his own crew, giving no explanation for his change of plan. No one made the mistake of asking.

No longer hindered by the reluctant herd, they were able to make better time, though it would have been impossible to face the teeth of the blizzard except for the rising light as dawn broke. Gradually the storm slackened. The snow had almost stopped by the time they reached the ranch buildings. Horses stumbling with weariness, the day drawing to its end, Slash and his men could barely stumble from barn to bunkhouse. Too exhausted to cook and eat a meal, they threw themselves on bunks to the oblivion of sleep.

Sun was in his face, slanting in at a window, when Slash awakened. Momentarily he was too stiff and sore, his mind still drugged with sleep, to think or understand. Then he realized that it was

close to noon—two days since the storm began—
the sun high in a cloudless sky, dazzling on the
endless snow fields that were just beginning to
melt.

It was an effort to convince himself that the
memory was not a bad dream, that the nightmar-
ish events had really happened. McKay had turned
up with his crew in time to save his herd, and by
now they would be returning the stock to their own
range—a weary chore, but under the circumstances, reason for elation.

Not to be overlooked was the certainty that
McKay knew—as he had somehow discovered or
guessed in time to take counteraction—that Slash,
his enemy, had been responsible for their wander-
ing.

Some of his crew would have recognized Slash.
Glimpsing him was not proof that he was a rustler
or reason enough to hang a man. But the less-than-
friendly relations between the two outfits, held to a
tenuous sort of neutrality while Longpre Connor
had lived, were irrevocably broken.

A streamer of smoke was beginning to crawl
upward from the cookhouse. Like himself, his
crew would be ravenous. It was a full two days
since they had eaten or enjoyed hot food washed
down by hot coffee.

Tugging on his boots, Slash's impulse was to
cross to the bunkhouse, to share in the meal, again

delaying, putting off the reality he must face for an extra hour or so. Then he caught a sound, a light step in another part of the house. That would be Cleo.

He was too deeply involved to turn back, but the game was not yet lost and might be won. Stealthily he slipped into the kitchen, where the big range poured out a pleasant heat against the continuing chill. The teakettle at the back of the stove sang softly. Filling a basin, he ducked back to his own room, then scraped away the accumulation of grime and whiskers from days on the trail. Surveying himself in the mirror, he was almost pleased.

The others, still unshaven, were at breakfast when he took his place at the table—a silent meal in which they wolfed their food and waited for orders that did not come. Glancing through a window, Slash saw a horseman pulling up, the cayuse splashing through suddenly sloppy snow. And though the afternoon sun disclaimed storm and darkness, the rider was a renewal of nightmare. Grubby Sanders was back.

He loomed in the doorway, a man shifting from the sheepishness of a cur fearing a kick to the arrogance of new-found power. His grin was a taunt.

"You fellows look like you'd had a rough time, battlin' the blizzard. Hell of a lot of damage everywhere, from all I hear an' see. That big cottonwood in town broke—smashed part of the Mercantile and plumb ruined the post office." His malicious grin was meaningful. "Thought I'd look in on you, Connor—make sure everything was fine, for such an old friend."

Slash controlled the impulse to curse and kick him out. The easy solution of a couple of days before had melted and his plight, bad as it had been, verged on the desperate. He jerked his head toward a side room.

"Since you're here, we might as well visit a spell," he managed with an amiability so false as to deceive no one. "I'll bring along a pot of coffee."

With the door closed, he poured fresh cups, shoving one at the clerk, cursing the proprietor of a store who would hire such dubious help. Cheapness was always undependable.

"The storm's kept me too busy, looking after the stock, to think or tend to anything else." That was true enough.

"Sure, I reckon so," Grubby conceded. "Mighty bad storm for any time of year, special for late summer. I didn't want to bother you till it was over," he added meaningly.

"Like I say, I've had no time to tend to anything else," Slash repeated. "It'll take me a few days to get that money together."

Grubby was falsely jovial.

"Just so you *do* get it," he agreed. "That's what I'm interested in." The little, close-set eyes matched a fox's. "Just so it's prompt, I might return you a little dividend. I've been hearing a funny sort of story—about a strayed herd that might maybe have turned into a stolen one, and folks makin' the funny mistake of thinkin' they saw *you* with it, through the storm...."

He paused to allow that, with its wider implications, to sink in, smirking.

"Crazy, ain't it, the notions some people get? Likely they'd realize how that was a mistake if I was to make mention how I'd talked with you over a game of cards at my place at just about that same time—a long day's ride in the opposite direction!"

20

Unending night and the weariness of storm and trail imposed a crushing burden. McKay was jerked from near-somnolence by O'Donnell's startled exclamation.

"Slash Connor! The damned cow thief! And high-tailin' it like the sneakin' coyote he is! Maybe I can bring him down—oh, hell! Blasted rifle's frozen solid."

Quick to understand and get the picture, McKay realized that Slash had been surprised, almost caught in the act with the stolen herd. Now he was beating a hasty retreat before the seething anger of the rightful owners. His presence at such a time and place supplied the final bit of solid evidence to the plot that had been complete in McKay's mind.

Chilled almost to exhaustion, he felt a satisfying lift. Handicapped he was, perhaps doomed to go sightless all his days, but he had demonstrated that he was still capable of running his ranch, of rising to emergencies. He had led his men when without him they would have been helpless, saving his herd from a ruinous loss. And he was enduring the blizzard's cold as well as any.

"Let them go," he said wearily. "Not much chance of finding them again in this storm. And you boys will have your hands full, turning the herd and getting them home. Hold them till the storm lets up, then bring them in."

That would probably be a three-day job. Close to exhaustion from their long trek, the cattle would have to rest, then take it easy on the route back home. The chief difference was that there would be a chance to graze as the snow melted.

Toby was chosen to return with McKay, serving as guide. With improving conditions, McKay's sense of direction would be rendered all but useless.

Slash held himself in check, studying Sanders with a sense of irony. Because for the moment he had the upper hand, Grubby deluded himself with the belief that he could maintain it. His offer to say that Slash had been a long ride from the strayed herd was too clumsy a bait, amounting to mockery. Told by such a man, it would fool no one.

"I've work to do," Slash informed him tersely. "And the longer I'm kept from it, the longer it will take me to tend to other matters."

"Sure, sure. I wouldn't keep you from such chores." Sanders was in high good humor. He and Shaney, the former cook at Lost Horse, were surprisingly alike both as to name and nature. Fate seemed to plague him in being forced to work with inept fools.

But that, Slash was discovering, was the price for dealing with men of no scruple, eager to be cheaply bought. Well, Grubby might delude himself that he held the whip hand. He was due for a rude awakening.

Alone, Slash felt a return of good humor. Bad luck had crowded him increasingly, but in one sense it was good. He was compelled to take the course from which he had shrunk, to make use of the one way that could solve his problems. But even now the prospect was like taking bitter medicine, however great his need for its cure. Since he had no other choice, he could delay no longer.

Cleo was eating her dinner, simple fare on a single plate at the kitchen table. She looked up as Slash entered the room, her gaze remote, almost detached. He had hoped for warmth or concern after so long an absence, but there was not even sisterly concern in her eyes. Then he reminded himself that they were still almost strangers, and there might be unanswered questions and doubts in her mind. It was up to him to dissipate them.

"I waited, thinking we might eat together," she observed. "But when you didn't come..."

"I had to see a man on business," Slash blurted. The idea of playing the host, of dining with his sister, had not occurred to him. The trouble, he realized, was that he was abashed, unsure of himself, ill at ease in this woman's presence. It was a sensation new and humbling. He pulled out a chair, seating himself opposite.

"I'm sorry," he added. "If I'd known—it would have been a lot nicer to eat with you. We—we need to talk things over. To—to get a few matters straightened out."

Cleo sipped her coffee, offering no help. Still with the sense of being a guest, though hardly a welcome one, she had made the first overture. The next move was up to him.

She sensed an approaching showdown in his manner and was increasingly apprehensive. Without knowing what to expect from her unknown relatives, nothing had turned out as she had imagined. She had been treated politely, but otherwise ignored, left to amuse herself or mope in isolation. The sense of being unwanted had grown with each day.

Yet, disregarded and isolated, she had picked up something of the background of this Triple Cross Ranch, with the connotation of such a brand; apparently the isolation she felt had applied to her father and brother, men without friends, unpredictably strange.

Slash waited hopefully, but as she made no response, no move to help him, he plunged ahead. Like the fox, he was devious by nature, but prone to strike with a matching directness when prey was cornered or helpless.

"I've been trying to figure out what to say, or how to say it," he blurted. "It's not easy. There's been a lot of—well, not just misunderstanding. It's worse than that."

"What do you mean?"

"Something I didn't know about, or even suspect, until a few weeks ago. I never knew about you, Cleo, or even much about myself, until Pa was hurt and dying. When he realized that he was going, he told me a few things. I guess some of them must have been bothering him for a long while, but he'd more or less been caught in his own trap."

"How—what do you mean?" Cleo repeated. She was interested now.

"I mean that you aren't really my sister. We aren't related. Your folks—your dad and brother—came west as you know about, heading for California. But your father had a change of heart, or at least of mind, so that he tried to do what your mother had wanted. Somewhere he made a deal for this ranch. Then he wrote a letter to your mother, telling her about it, wanting her to come out with you and join him here."

Despite the bluntness of the assertion, like a slap in the face, Cleo was not much surprised. For the first time, this history held a certain amount of reason.

"But if he did that, then how—"

"What he planned didn't work out. He died of the plague—cholera. Thousands did. He and your brother. After that, my pa helped himself to their wagon and outfit, and of course he read the letter. Instead of mailing it, he took your father's name, then came and claimed the ranch. I've always supposed that Connor was my name. I don't even know what my pa's might have been."

Slash was being as truthful as possible. He drew a long breath.

"Sure it was a sneaking, dirty deal, though I can understand it. I never knew anything about it, until just about the time you were to arrive. I didn't know what to do or how to treat you. That's why I didn't meet the stage. But now, I'm sure glad that you aren't my sister. For that leaves us free to get married."

"To—to get married!" Her gasp was incredulous, but Slash was too full of his own thoughts to notice.

"Sure. That will straighten everything out, at least as far as it's possible to make matters right after what has happened. And I'm crazy about you, Cleo. You're the only woman I've ever cared about—"

He checked, incredulous, unwilling to believe, but with suddenly sharpened perceptions he could not misunderstand. Cleo was shrinking away, the abhorrence on her face and manner vivid. There was no need to ask what her answer would be.

21

Night brooded like a great bird over the range, its gloom somewhat lightened by the snow that still blanketed the ground and by high stars. The recent blizzard, as though repenting of its surprise visit, had departed, leaving it to time and man to pick up the pieces.

Cleone, moving in a frozen calmness that matched the crusting snow, rolled and tied a hasty bundle of possessions, an inadequate selection from the baggage she had brought to the ranch not long before. She would miss and probably need what was left behind, but it was impossible to take more on a horse at such short notice. Whether it might be possible to send back for the rest seemed doubtful, but she had no choice.

She could not remain at Triple Cross after what had happened, coupled with Slash Connor's wild declarations. She did not doubt that he was telling the truth, and for the first time she had some understanding for her father and sympathy for him. Far from a callous disregard for his wife and daughter, he had been working to correct mistakes, pursuing a middle course he had hoped would be acceptable to her mother. Contrary to what she and her mother had supposed, he had not forgotten or been heartlessly neglectful.

Such knowledge was comforting, but at the moment it was a pitifully small measure to set against her plight and that of Dave McKay. Slash's declaration of love and his intention to marry her had been more terrifying than his previous neglect. This pair, father and son, who had stolen her father's name along with his land, were a wild breed, as driven by circumstance as the Lost Horse herd stumbling before the push of the blizzard.

That the ranch belonged to her, not partially but

totally, only worsened the situation. Rage as well as incredulity had twisted Slash's face as her fear and hate had become clear. Her rejection was a fresh stab to his already lacerated pride, and coupled with the certainty that only by marrying her could he keep control of the ranch, his reaction was certain.

For the moment he was uncertain of how best to proceed but felt no great sense of urgency. But there was no telling how long that might last. She must escape, get away while she could.

Only when she had saddled a horse did it come to her that she had nowhere to go, no place to turn—except for Dave McKay at the Lost Horse. She was thankful that the darkness hid the rising color that enveloped her throat and face as she thought of him. That was the answer. She would be welcome there, and safe. And they were in this together, sharing a mutual peril as the objects in the way of Slash Connor's ambition.

Alone under the stars, she admitted the truth. She was going to Dave not only because there was nowhere else to go, but because she was sure of a welcome—because she loved him. Again her cheeks flamed, then she threw back her head with conscious pride. She was not going as a supplicant or beggar. Her lawful holdings made a rich dowery.

The snow, which had measured up to twenty

inches where it had lain unmolested by the wind, had compressed to less than a quarter of that depth. She had no difficulty in following the roads, avoiding the more direct and frightening pass taken by Baldy O'Brion, where it twisted toward the stars. Even that trip seemed remote and far removed.

No lights showed as she approached the ranch buildings at Lost Horse, and she was momentarily apprehensive and at a loss. The hour was not overly late. Then she remembered snatches of conversation she had overheard from the Triple Cross men of how McKay's herd had drifted with the storm. The crew would be rounding them up, and it would take at least another day to get them back.

With the crew away, Dave was probably alone. He would strike no light, moving as he did in a sightless world. In the desolation of such a picture, Cleo's heart seemed to fill her throat. But now she had the means to combat his pride, to serve to some extent in place of the eyes he had lost.

She unsaddled and stabled her horse, forced to fumble uncertainly in the vast, empty barn, reminded anew of what life was like for McKay. How he had managed to adjust so well, to keep going under such a handicap, excited admiration along with pity. Though where such a man was concerned, the latter emotion was out of place.

She found her legs suddenly shaky as she paused at the door of the house. It took a moment to gather her courage before she could knock. She was sure that what she was doing was right and proper for both of them, and necessary, but that did not make it easy.

The great bulk of this house loomed even larger by night than in daylight. And big was the word. The purpose in building on so large a scale could only be guessed. Solid and fortlike, it came to her that the protective aspect had not been overlooked. Undoubtedly in those days there had been the possibility, even the risk, of Indian attack.

Whatever the reasons, the house sprawled, solidly massive. Most of its rooms were unused, rarely opened—more than ever now that McKay was alone and sightless. And yet what possibilities such a house held as a home!

Her knuckles sounded loud against the silence of the night. Then there was a step, certain yet curiously hesitant, and a voice as the knob turned: "Who's there?"

"It's me, David—Cleo. I had to come—"

"Cleo—you!" He breathed her name like a benediction. "I was sittin' here, dreaming about you." His voice was pleased, strangely awed. "Come in. I'll get a light."

She heard him move, this time with certainty. "I'm all alone here," he added. "The crew are with the herd, and they won't likely be back for at least another day."

"That doesn't matter," she said and repeated, "I had to come."

While he got a lamp alight she told him what Slash had confessed a few hours before, even to his eagerness to marry her.

"Of course that's what he'd want. My being his wife would give him a legal title to Triple Cross, and that is the only way he could hold it. He wants to complete the steal his father started.

"Actually, I've no complaints about the way he's treated me, but each day, as I learned a little more, here and there, I've grown more and more frightened. After what happened, I didn't dare stay another night. I had to get away before he suspected that I might—and I had to warn you, David." Her voice rose on a sudden note of apprehension.

"I'm sure he'll try to hit at you again, to destroy you. I only hope he doesn't think to try before your men return."

With her revelations, the same thought had come to McKay. Slash had driven himself into a corner, and his confession to Cleo was an admission that he was in desperate straits. Had she consented to marry him, most of his difficulties would be over. Her refusal would both terrify and enrage him.

Cleone had shown excellent judgment as well as
courage in slipping away in the night. Her refusal
had surprised Slash, leaving him temporarily at a
loss, but reflection would render him desperate.
When desperate he abandoned devious scheming
and moved in the headlong charge of a mad bull.

This would be such an occasion. The only
question was what he might try, or the timing of
such attack. Believing Cleo safe in her room, he
might wait for daylight. That left the possibility
that McKay's crew would be back in time to assist.

But he might discover Cleo's absence. Then he
would almost certainly attempt to strike before
O'Donnell and the others could return.

Cleone was drawn and pale, desperately tired
from excitement and reaction. At McKay's
direction she lit another lamp, then, amazed at the
sureness with which he moved through the vast
and fearsome house, she followed as he led the
way. Soon he opened the door to a room
comfortably furnished with unmistakably femi-
nine daintiness.

"I think you'll be comfortable here," McKay
explained. "I had a neighbor lady come in and fix
it up nearly a year ago, when I thought a cousin
was coming to visit. She changed her mind at the
last moment, so you're its first guest. I'll be back
where I was, if you want anything. There's a bolt
on the door," he added.

"I won't need that," Cleo returned. "Not with you within call. Are you sure you can find your way back without any trouble? It's such a big place, and so—so dreadfully dark!"

"I'm used to both," he reassured her, then called from the gloom: "Sleep well. See you in the morning."

For himself, sleep was slow in coming. Knowing that she was in the house changed things. Her presence seemed somehow to permeate even the darkness. If she could only stay...And she had nowhere else to go! But to think along those lines was torment.

It was too bad that the special room was so remote, for she might find it frightening. Except for his cousin, he had never given much thought to what a woman would like.

McKay awoke with the realization that something unusual had roused him; it was a recurring nightmare, dreadfully familiar, unpleasantly similar to that initial awakening when the grizzly had prowled his camp.

As then, there was the crackling of flames, a reek of smoke. A blast of heat struck as he jerked upright. The house was on fire.

22

Pacing the confines of his own room in the manner of a caged bear, the notion came suddenly to Connor. Night-born, the solution was complete and total, satisfying in scope. Its result should be equally complete, leaving behind no evidence which might be traced. Fire!

His visits to Lost Horse had been furtive and far between, but he was familiar with the massive house. Its tinder-dry wood would burn readily, and tonight there would be no witnesses, not even a crew to battle the flames, however hopelessly. Nothing, in fact, to hinder the blaze.

He could pile dry wood at each corner and even points between, and have all of them ablaze in a matter of moments. McKay would be asleep inside. There would be nothing to hear, nor could he detect any warning glare of mounting flames. By the time he realized what was happening, it would be too late.

Some might harbor suspicions, after it was all over, but a guess was not proof. Once McKay was out of his way, he could take over, bringing an impossible situation under quick control.

Jealousy whispered the real reason why Cleo refused his attentions. It was suddenly clear enough. She had seen a lot more of McKay than himself since coming to this range, and she was always siding with the fellow! But once McKay was out of the way, she must see the hopelessness of refusing him.

Slash lost no time in making his preparations. He must be back in his own bed before another dawn, and that left no time for dawdling.

His mind worked as smoothly as the cylinder of a well-oiled Colt. There would be no dry wood in the wake of the storm, but it did not take long to bundle a supply from the firewood at his own cookhouse.

Each step fell smoothly into place. Blazes leaped to raging flames, fires licking at well-cured logs, crimson teeth gnawing greedily.

Withdrawing to a comfortable distance in deeper gloom, Slash kept watch, an easy matter in the spreading circle of light. Should McKay somehow manage to reach a door or window, he would get no farther.

But there was no reason for apprehension. Both doors, the unused front door at one side as well as the one to the kitchen, were seas of scarlet. From end to end, the vast pile was engulfed.

It was then that Slash heard the wild, high scream, a woman's cry of terror. Despite its quivering fear, he recognized the voice and froze. It was incredible, beyond belief, but it was the voice of the woman he had come to love. Somehow she was trapped by the flames he had set. For a moment he hesitated, striving to understand, then in a sudden frenzy he drove toward door or window, only to be forced back by ever-widening waves of intolerable heat.

The probable solution came to McKay as he jerked open his door, only to shrink back from a more intense blast of smoke and heat. Such fires did not happen by accident. And Cleo would long since have blown out her own lamp.

The answer was obvious, though Slash probably would not have guessed that Cleo might be a guest in this house. Undoubtedly he supposed her asleep in her own room, miles away.

The situation was desperate. He had to reach Cleo, then somehow get out before they suffocated or were trapped by collapsing walls and roof. McKay plunged through the wave of heat, moving almost at a run. Familarity and sharpened senses were at least as helpful as sight in such a stench. More heat choked, the smoke thickening, then subsiding.

Clearly, the arsonist had done a thorough job, setting several fires, all spreading and joining. Only the fact that they were set outside, slowed from breaking through by the thick walls, gave McKay any hope. But some of the flames were inside. Had he been able to see, McKay guessed grimly that he might have been turned back by aspects so terrifying as to daunt the strongest resolution.

Again there was a blast of heat. Then he was past it and beating on a door—it had to be her door, though under such conditions it was hard to be sure. It opened, and Cleo was clinging to him, frantic but not hysterical.

"Dave!" she breathed. "I knew you'd come. But there's fire at the window! I closed the shutter, but the flames are eating through. And there's fire just beyond you, in the hall!"

It was only what he had feared and expected. Desperately tired, she had slept overlong, too late to escape by door or window. Again he sensed that if he could see what was in their way he would lack the courage to try, but there was nothing to gain by hesitation.

"Wrap a blanket around yourself," he instructed. "Now hang onto my hand."

His plan was not so foolhardy as it appeared, and she obeyed. A swift, choking rush through frantic heat, then they turned a corner and conditions were bearable. He measured a few steps, then checked, fumbling for a door, for the knob. Beyond, as it opened, was darkness, suddenly total as he pulled it shut behind, but he was holding her hand, using his other to feel the way. As totally sightless as he, she marveled that it neither slowed nor hindered him.

They descended a flight of steps, then were on a level, with dirt underfoot and apparently at either side. She sensed that this was a tunnel back into the hill that a corner of the house bordered. McKay slowed and explained.

"This was dug a long while back, when the first small house was built—a chance to hide or escape in case of Indian attack. The outer door should be hereabouts."

Cleo felt a rush of hope. Then, like a beacon flaring only to subside, the hope ebbed. The door barring their way was massive. Iron-bound planks, long unused, refused to stir even after McKay managed to force back the rusty bolt.

The fire could not overtake them, but the smoke and gases from the inferno would follow relentlessly, as certain a peril as the flames unless they could get through the door and out.

McKay worked, tugging like a madman. He tore the tight-set door partly away, giving Cleo a glimpse of outer air, of a weird red glow reflected against the sky. The next instant the rotted frame, no longer bolstered, came crashing down, collapsing on and over them. For a second time in that nightmare of crimsoned darkness she screamed as they were trapped and held.

Half dazed, McKay struggled, but this time to no avail. Then another frantic pair of hands wrenched away a half-rotted upright where it tilted crazily, freeing Cleo so that she could move. She strained to aid McKay, only to be caught a second time by a torrent of dirt, loosened from its bracings and soaked by the melt of recent snow, cascading, overwhelming.

McKay lay limp and apparently lifeless as she finally clawed and scratched away dirt and a heavy wooden beam. Then she tugged, dragging him to the clear air beyond.

Dazedly she noticed something else, a second head and shoulders, limp and horribly smeared. Hopelessly trapped, Slash was mercifully dead beneath that final slide of rubble.

McKay stirred, moved gingerly, to stare in turn and shake his head.

"Reckon he heard you—and hadn't counted on you being caught. He sure enough saved us, there at the last. Which sort of cleans the slate."

Cleo was staring into his face, her hands on his arm, shaking impellingly.

"Dave! You're looking at him—you're seeing!"

McKay blinked, bemused. He *was* seeing—not too clearly, but beyond doubt. No longer drugged, his sight was returning. His arms went about a shaking Cleo, disregarding the crash of the collapsing house.

"You're right! And do you know—you're more'n twice as pretty than I remembered!"